Billionaire TAKES ALL

JACKSON KANE

------- HOT TREE PUBLISHING -------

"I must say, I COULDN'T PUT IT DOWN! I mean from the opening lines to the end, I was enraptured with the story."
-Moments in West FL book blog

"I just loved this book! You can feel the characters and you live the story. I will so be reading anything Jackson Kane writes."
-Beantown Bitches

"This story has so much chemistry that you could blow up a high school chemlab. This book had a great flow that kept me the reader devouring every page. The combination of humor, love, sex and a little dramatic action gives this book a solid 5 Star review from me."
-Alpha Book Club

"... it was a strong debut from a very lovely author, and I can't wait to see what comes next."
-Summer's Eve Reads

"Jackson Kane's does a really great job of sucking you into this book."
-Tasty WordGasms.

Billionaire Takes All is a work of fiction. All names, characters, events and places found therein are either from the author's imagination or used fictitiously. Any similarity to persons alive or dead, actual events, locations, or organizations is entirely coincidental and not intended by the author.

For information, contact the publisher, Hot Tree Publishing.
WWW.HOTTREEPUBLISHING.COM

EDITING: HOT TREE EDITING
COVER DESIGNER: BOOKSMITH DESIGN
FORMATTING: RMGRAPHX

E-BOOK ISBN: 978-1-922359-09-4
PAPERBACK ISBN: 978-1-922359-10-0

PROLOGUE

Lucas

I just lost my half of five billion dollars.

Five. Billion. Fucking. dollars.

I crushed the phone in my hand, but the voice mail chimed in my brain like church bells at midnight. It was probably the same message my brother just got.

"Your father is dying. The inheritance is no longer yours *or* your brother's. If you want a chance at that money, you're going to have to play by some... unconventional rules."

Rules? Fuck that!

I didn't get this far by following *anyone's* rules.

"Only one of you can win," the message said. "The other gets nothing."

But I did know one thing: if this really was a competition between my brother and me for the whole King fortune, *I was going to win.*

That was probably exactly what Richard was saying right then too. He and I hated each other; we had for years.

With my hand throbbing, I flexed my fingers. The final sentence of that damn message had flipped my life upside down and kicked it down the fucking sidewalk.

"Good luck, Lucas. You're going to need it."

One thing's for sure, our sleepy town of Caldwell Hope is in for a rude awakening.

When the King brothers come back home, all hell's breaking loose.

CHAPTER 1

Lucas

"Excuse me." The woman's voice was as sweet and distant as a pleasant dream.

Grass beneath me, the sounds of cars busily rushing by, the briskly intermittent breeze and the bathing warmth of the sun.

Fuck, I was outside.

I hated waking up outside.

The birds were the worst pressure point on my massive hangover. Their sharp tweets cut through my ears like an ice pick.

"Hello, shirtless man? You can't be here," said the voice more insistently. Was I still dreaming? It sounded way too familiar to be anything but a dream.

I covered my face, fighting the waking world, determined to go back to sleep. I had no idea what time it was, but I knew that it was way too damn early for me to be coherent.

"Excuse me," the woman repeated, getting closer. She was trying to hide the bookish timidity from her voice.

That voice was crazy familiar....

"For Christ's sake, you're excused." I grumbled as loudly as I could, shifting my arm to further shield my face from the relentless sunlight. "Now let me sleep."

She scoffed at my bluntness.

The kick in the ribs I received wasn't bookish or sweet.

"Fuck me, that's a rude way to treat a guest." I recoiled, rolling away onto my stomach. My long, dirty-blond hair cascaded down both sides of my face as I lifted myself from a push up position. Once I got my knees under me, I shot a quick glance at her, but my eyes hadn't adjusted fully, so I only caught a glimpse before the intensity of the sun forced me to look away.

Her long, layered, brown hair had soft curls and was pulled back into a ponytail. She had a slight, yet athletic frame, and wore a gray dress. Was that the glint of glasses I saw?

Wasn't the girl last night a redhead? I also didn't remember her being this gorgeous....

"Rude? Guest?" Her tone screamed *the gall of this man!*

That didn't make any sense. I distinctly remember being invited to the party last night by a few fans. They wanted me here. Why was I being yelled at?

My ears were still faintly humming from all the music I had played.

I carelessly rubbed my sore chest and abs to get off the matted grass and dirt. It was a useless effort; all my tattoos made the mess impossible to see, let alone brush off. I desperately needed a shower. I cocked my head to the side, and through my hanging hair caught the pretty brunette gawking.

She could try to hide it, but I could tell that she liked what she saw. *Damn right,* I thought. *I don't work out five times a week to not look good.*

"Yeah, *guest*. You invited me." My long hair blanketed my head like an overturned mop. With the speed and precision of someone who was just hit by a car, I grabbed the wadded fabric in my back pocket and pulled out a purple G-string. "These are yours, aren't they?"

"Eww, no! And this is school property. *No one* invited you to sleep here!"

"What?" I flipped my hair back and took in the surroundings. If they weren't hers, then where the hell was I?

The long, rectangular building loomed nearby, obviously some kind of school. I spotted the playground peeking out from the back of the nicely remodeled building.

Oh wonderful. I'm shirtless and reeking of booze in front of an elementary school. Definitely not one of the high points of my life.... *Yeah, this won't make it into my autobiography.* I was glad it was Saturday.

At least I hoped it was Saturday....

Either way, there were no children around, thankfully. Although, I'd probably make a good example of what not to do when you grow up.

Then it got worse. I spotted the name on the building—Matt Baker Elementary school. *Matt Baker.* That's where I was?

"Oh shit…," I muttered. That's why she looked and sounded so familiar.

"Your eyes... hazel," she said in wistful tones, not trusting her own eyes.

My face puckered up, and my eyes clamped shut as if bracing for a hit. Stupidity always hurt much more than physical pain. Of all the places I could've drunkenly stumbled last night, why'd I pick here?

I fucked up. *Bad.*

"Luke?" Molly Baker gasped, the dream of her past finally becoming real.

Just waking up, being hungover and crashing in an unfamiliar place was a perfect storm for my brain to be a fucking wreck. Still... there was no excuse. I should've known much sooner.

I'd heard that voice every night while I slept for ten long years.

I snapped my eyes open and saw her. *Really saw her.* Suddenly I was as awake as someone who got a shot of adrenaline straight to the vein. My heart began to claw its way into the back of my throat.

It really was her....

She was impossibly prettier than I remembered.

"Molly." The name tumbled from my lips. I needed a few more *lifetimes* to figure out what to say to her. *I'm sorry. I didn't know. It wasn't my choice to leave you. Every day I wanted to come back for you.*

Every single day.

I knew every inch of Molly's sun-kissed skin and the way her light freckles were only visible in some light. Her lips were glossy pink pillows made of clouds on a perfect afternoon, and her eyes were the color of amber at dusk.

I'd always thought about what this moment would be like if it ever happened. I'd planned it a thousand times in a thousand ways. Sometimes she'd be walking by when I'd stop her and tell her how much I missed her. Other times I'd just show up at her door and ask her out so I could explain everything. Every time I met her in my head, it was on my terms and usually with a bouquet of flowers.

So much for best laid plans....

I *at least* thought I'd have more clothes on when we met.

"Molly, I—" The crack of her knuckles stole the rest of my sentence and snapped my head back.

"Ow, shit. That hurt!" Molly's arm recoiled. She scowled, shaking the pain out of her hand.

"Okay, I deserved that." I wiped the blood trickling down my nose. It was a good punch, but she didn't break anything. It did however kick my headache into overdrive. Fortunately it wasn't anything I couldn't handle. Especially not when there was so much to say.

"Where'd you learn how to punch like that?"

"I picked up a few things in the ten years since you abandoned me." Molly rubbed her sore knuckles.

"Molly, I'm—"

"Don't you dare." She balled her fists back up. Was she going to punch me for trying to apologize? "You don't get to do that. You can't just roll into town without a word, say you're sorry, and expect everything to be forgiven."

"This wasn't the way I was hoping this would go." I licked the blood off my teeth and wiped my mouth and light beard again.

"We don't always get what we want, do we?" Her beautiful brown eyes narrowed. "I see you've stayed busy." Her eyes flicked down to the thong in my fist.

"These aren't mine." I sighed. *No shit.* "I mean, these aren't what you think—"

I wish I wasn't so hungover. This looked much worse than it was. The redhead at the party stuffed them into my pocket and said they were the key to her bedroom. I left shortly after that. I never made it into the house, let alone her bedroom. I definitely never touched her.

"You know what? I don't even want to know."

Fuck!

There was no way Molly would believe what really happened. I was a rock star with all the trappings—

fans, groupies, the whole nine yards....

Hell, *I* wouldn't believe me.

What no one knew was that getting underwear thrown at me was a surprisingly common occurrence. Sometimes it didn't even happen while I was on stage. There's another side to fame that no one gives a shit about.

The sad, honest truth was that I hadn't had sex with anyone in a long time.

I looked around for a trash can and saw one near where my bike was parked, but I wasn't ready to leave things like this with Molly. I shoved the panties back into my pocket.

What else could I do? I wasn't about to throw them on the lawn of an elementary school, especially not one named after her dead brother.

"The new school looks nice." I began to remember how I got here. This was my first stop when I came into town last night. I heard the renovations were finally finished, and I had to see it with my own eyes.

"Anonymous donation. It turns out there are nice, thoughtful people in the world after all."

"Yeah… I'm sorry to hear about Matt."

"Don't. Just…." Molly took a deep breath and exhaled. "I want you to go, Luke."

"Molly. Wait a second." I took a step in and grabbed her arms. Her perfume wafted up between us. She smelled like heaven. Now that she was so close, it was hard to stop myself from hugging her like when we were kids.

If I did that, I'd never be able to let her go.

Why couldn't we have that again?

I could see the spark in her eyes, and it wasn't just because I was half naked. I knew *those* looks. I saw them all the time from girls that only saw me as a rock star or as a ripped piece of meat.

Molly's was different.

Yeah, I could feel her pulse and breath racing. I knew she was still attracted to me, but there was so much more in those brown eyes. There was pissed-off anger and pain. And beyond that there was something else.

There was still a glimmer of the girl I used to know back before it all fell to shit.

And I could never truly give up on that girl. *Ever.*

Her expression softened, and her eyes turned up, then closed. She was allowing herself to *just feel.* So much time had passed, but what we had was truly special. You couldn't just recover from something like that.

It stayed with you for the rest of your life.

"A day hasn't gone by where I didn't think about you." The distance between us evaporated like boiling water. "I'm so sorry I had to leave."

"This time don't come back." Molly pulled her arms away at the last moment and turned her back on me. "I've moved on."

Molly walked away from me.

CHAPTER 2

Richard

"Greetings, Mr. King. I'll be your driver for the duration of your stay in Caldwell Hope." The driver introduced himself once I stepped out of the open door.

I nodded in acknowledgment, and he immediately began loading my luggage from my jet into the short white limo.

Even through my dark sunglasses, my eyes needed a moment to adjust against the midday glare that boiled off the runway's tarmac. The cloudless sun turned my throbbing hangover into a stabbing spike.

I desperately needed coffee.

I snapped open the top button of my collared shirt. It was hot in a way that only the southwestern states got in late spring. It was probably going to be a scorcher of a summer.

Fortunately I wouldn't be here long enough to find out.

My driver finished with the luggage, then straightened his posture and opened the limo door for me. He thoughtfully added, "Welcome home, sir."

"Home." I rolled the word around in my mouth like an expensive wine that was too bitter for my palate. *Not for me. Not anymore.*

Once this meeting with my father and brother was finished, Caldwell Hope would go back to being a place I rarely thought about and never visited.

The lovely British flight attendant leaned against the doorway wearing only a towel and a satisfied smile. My white Panama hat hung limply in her hand. She was a talented girl and was just what I needed to make the trip back here tolerable.

I gave her an easy smile and a kiss on the cheek, then took the hat and put it on. That was better. I straightened my vest and brushed down my tailored pants, then stepped into the air-conditioned car. With a good hat and a nice watch, I could be buck naked and still feel comfortable.

"Are you from around here, James?" I asked the chauffeur. He was surprisingly young. I was thirty-one, and this was the first time I'd ever had a driver who was younger than me.

"Yes, sir. Born and raised."

"Fantastic. Do you know the way to the Village Bean? I need a coffee." There was no way I was going to deal with whatever my father had in store for us without some caffeine to clear my head. "Call me

Richard. I get enough 'sirs' at the office."

"I'm sorry, s—" James had to catch himself as it probably went against everything he'd been taught. "The Village Bean closed about ten years ago I believe. I know another place that's just as good, if you'd like."

Ten years? Had I really been gone that long? I quickly did the math and realized it was actually longer than that.

What else had changed?

I agreed, and James drove us into town. My quiet little prison had apparently flourished over the years and became quite the vacation spot. The familiar low mountains framed the downtown strip, but almost everything else had changed or been updated.

Bouquets of pink and white flowers hung in the rough-hewn brick buildings that connected several trendy-looking shops. The whole area, down to the signage, had a unified, quaint theme about it.

It had certainly grown more charming in my absence.

We slowed to a stop outside a record store. I was about to ask him about it when I spotted the A-shaped sign on the sidewalk in front of the store. "Black Rocket Records," the sign said.

Beneath that it bragged, "We dare you to find a better damn cup of coffee."

The place had style. That's for sure.

James asked what he could get for me, but I waved him off. The record store had piqued my interest, and after the long flight, I wanted to stretch my legs anyway.

I took my hat and sunglasses off as I walked in. Black Rocket Records was more than just its namesake. There were racks of old books, records, novelties, coffee bar, and even a stage for live music. Teenagers' paradise.

Heads started turning, and a few people stepped out of my way. It might have been a long time since I'd been back here, but people had TVs and smartphones. They knew who I was.

I smiled back at a few pretty girls and shook one guy's hand who let me cut in front of him at the coffee line. I wasn't looking for special treatment, but who was I to say no? The line was only a few people long, and no one else seemed to have a problem with it, so I stepped up to the ordering station.

"Hello?" I asked, looking around. The wall behind the register was lined with all sorts of fancy presses, slow drips, steamers, and brewing stations. They were all actively in the process of doing… something.

I leaned forward, resting my cufflinks atop a glass countertop—which encapsulated an elaborate collage of Alice in Wonderland pictures—and asked again, louder this time.

It was all very trendy, but where was the barista?

"One second!" a strained female voice sharply called up from beneath the bar. "How many?"

"I'd like a coffee?" Why would they want to know how many before what kind?

"Yeah, no shit. How many?" the annoyed voice

snapped back.

I cocked an eyebrow at the rudeness of the disembodied voice. I couldn't even remember the last time someone took that tone with me. *No, thanks,* I thought, prepping to leave. *There are plenty of other coffee places in town.*

I was in the process of turning to leave when the barista finally popped straight up with a stack of cups in each arm.

She was short, petite, had a shock of short black hair, and was pale enough to make a vampire envious. She wore a faded black, obscure band T-shirt, had glittering studs running up both her ears, and eye shadow dark enough to drain the light from the room.

I'd never been into the alt-rock girls, but right away I could tell there was something very different about this one.

I glanced down her slight form for a name tag, but of course she didn't have one. Maybe it was that she was so far from the perfect blonde Hollywood type that got my blood pumping. Or maybe it was her eyes. She had these light gray irises that crackled like storm clouds before a hard rain.

Suddenly coffee was the last thing on my mind. Who was this girl?

"Well?" the barista asked impatiently, wiping the sweat from her face with the crook of her elbow.

"Caffè macchiato—" I started my order, but was quickly interrupted with an annoyed look and an upraised index finger.

I followed the pointing gesture to a sign above her head that read, "Coffee made our way. Deal with it."

"Are you always this rude? Or am I just the lucky punching bag today?"

The barista narrowed her eyes. "That's kind of our whole deal here. That and I don't like those who cut in line."

How had she even seen me? Was she part ninja?

I was just about to protest that they all let me pass when a tall blonde woman stepped up behind the barista, cutting her off.

"Hi there! I'm Judy." She was as chipper as the dark-haired girl was not. It was a stark contrast. "I saw your interview on the *Late Show*. You did such a good job. So handsome in that pinstripe suit! It's so nice to meet you! We're more of a self-serve kind of place, but we can make an exception for one of the *Kings* of Caldwell Hope. That was a caffè macchiato, right?"

Her voice was cotton candy, and her cadence was rapidly popping popcorn. Did this woman ever breathe? Now I desperately needed the coffee just to follow this conversation.

"Hi." I squeezed the greeting in somewhere between her flood of words. "Yes, ma'am."

"Gloria makes it much better than I could ever dream of!" Judy switched from me to her raven-haired partner. "Would you mind?" She held up her hands in a pleading motion then mouthed the word "Please."

I smiled at their unlikely dynamic. It was obvious that they were peers, probably co-owners.

How did that work?

I couldn't imagine two people more different. They were the sun and the moon.

Gloria sighed at Judy's cheeriness, then walked off toward the self-service station without giving me another glance. I couldn't take my eyes off her as she left. When she stepped out from the bar, I could see her midthigh-length black skirt and milky, smooth legs.

The sight of her slight form swaying got my blood pumping.

Judy told me the coffee was on the house, then asked for a selfie with me. I obliged, distractedly. I caught Gloria looking over at me discretely as she made my coffee. It gave me an unexpected thrill. I might have to come back here and see her again before I flew out of town.

"Here," Gloria said, handing me the drink. Her voice had a bite to it that deepened my smirk. "*Your Majesty.*"

I thought about getting Gloria's number, but when I looked up she was already ringing out another customer. I slipped a fifty into the tip jar and flashed Gloria a wink; then I left.

Outside James waited with his arms behind his back. He opened the car door for me as I approached. The coffee smelled delicious but was still too hot to drink. I peeled the cover off to help it cool faster and slowed to a stop when I saw the design.

"Is everything all right?" James asked, easily seeing the intrigued expression on my face. "I hope there wasn't a mix-up."

In the brown and white of the foamed-milk-topped coffee was the artistically drawn image of a cock and balls, throbbing veins and all.

"No." I glanced back through the glass doors and took a scalding sip. Her outline was clear in the lit room. The glare and the distance made it impossible to make out her stormy eyes, but I had the feeling that Gloria was still watching me. I smiled as I looked at her. "This one has my name written all over it."

CHAPTER 3

Lucas

Pulling up to my father's fifty-million-dollar mansion, I was reminded just how different I was from the rest of the family.

The sprawling stone and glass building was beautifully integrated into the gently sloping hill at the far end, giving it a natural look and blending it into the lush green surroundings nearly seamlessly.

An unbroken view of Caldwell Hope stretched out in the valley below in all its glory. Blue-tipped mountains seemed to cradle the property and framed the house in a way that would make postcards jealous.

This was a castle fit for a king who liked to watch over his kingdom.

I slowed my bike as I crested the driveway and made my way toward the garage and main entrance. There was no front yard. Instead, there was a massive man-made pond and waterfall. The early afternoon was cloudy enough that the accent lighting that ran up each pillar was visible in the shimmering water before it, making the already huge house look much bigger.

If you could hire God for architecture side work, this was what he'd build.

I killed the engine and sighed at the picturesque tranquility of it all. Yeah, it was pretty. All of it was super impressive... *in a fucking useless and selfish way.*

So much money wasted that could've been put to better use.

Of course, I didn't think that way when Molly and I were lovestruck kids and I was trying to impress her. That was a lifetime ago when everything made sense. Seventeen years old and we had it all figured out.

We were going to be together forever.

Forever wasn't as long as it used to be....

No matter how far I ran, thoughts of Molly were always just a heartbeat away. I clenched my jaw at the familiar pain. Seeing her today was going to fuck with me for a long time.

I hadn't been here a full day yet, and I already wished I'd never come back.

"Greetings, Mr. King," the young valet called out from the opening garage door and rushed out to meet me. My father's extensive classic car collection glistened against the polished white floors and overhead lights. It was less a garage and more of a showroom.

I snorted out a chuckle. Here I was, *a billionaire*

heir, and the only vehicle I owned at the moment was a motorcycle.

"Hey, kid. You got an extra shirt?" I laid my jacket over the bike's seat and stretched out the road soreness. It was too warm for thick leather when I wasn't riding.

"I don't think so, but I can have someone pick one up for you."

"It's cool. Don't worry about it." I checked my phone. I was only about two hours late for lunch. Not bad for me.

What the fuck happened to my shirt? At some point last night I lost it, but when?

"Uh, sir?" The apprehension in the way the valet looked at my bike was clear as day. His job was to park and maintain *cars*. He probably had no idea what to do with my beat-up motorcycle. It didn't help that I'd parked it in the dead middle of the driveway, blocking the easiest path into one of the garage bays.

"Leave it." I shrugged off his concern, spotting my brother Richard, who'd just stepped out the front door on his phone. I walked toward the inevitable argument. "I won't be staying long."

Richard hung up the phone as I ascended the final steps to the front door landing. We stood there for a long moment, sizing each other up. Even in the growing heat of late spring, Richard was immaculately manicured in his expensive three-piece suit.

"You're late," he said, behind thick sunglasses. He crossed his arms disapprovingly and flashed an expression that said he wasn't impressed. Richard was tall, clean shaven, and had a pretentious side fade and short shock-top hairstyle that was all the rage these days.

He looked like someone smashed together the covers of GQ and Forbes magazines.

"That depends on your perspective." My posture stiffened, chest out, shoulders rolled back. He might've been able to make lawyers and other CEOs piss themselves, but he'd never been able to intimidate me. "I got here exactly when I wanted to."

We both had the same color hair and eyes, but other than that, we couldn't be any more different. He was taller than me, but I was more muscular. If it ever came down to it, I'd take him apart in a real fight.

"You expect the world to adjust itself to your every whim."

"I don't expect a damn thing from anyone." I shrugged. "I just do what I want."

"They say that every seven years each cell in your body has been replaced. You're an entirely new person. So why is it that I'm still talking to a seventeen-year-old boy who still can't handle a shred of responsibility like arriving somewhere on time?"

My brother was such a judgmental prick. He'd made it perfectly clear that I was wrong for doing my own thing. I didn't want college or grad school; I wanted music. I didn't want to be groomed to fall in line with the family business like some good little duckling. I wanted to tour with my band.

"Spare me your fortune cookie wisdom. Ten years later, you're still a dick, *Dick*." It'd been at least that long since we had an actual conversation, but from the look on his face, I could tell he still didn't like the nickname. "Growing up doesn't mean putting on an overpriced suit and firing people."

"This is coming from a guy who doesn't even have a shirt. You lose it in a fight or a card game?"

"Dunno. Last night was pretty hazy. Whatever happened, I'm sure it was a hell of a good time." When given the option, it was impossible for me not to try and rile him up. There was brotherly love, but this was more like brotherly hate. "It's called fun; you should give it a shot some time."

"Dad's not going to be around forever. Some day you're going to have to man up and make something of yourself."

"What do you call two number one hits then?" Nothing I ever did was good enough for Richard. Success was only measured on his terms.

"Where's your band now?"

"Fuck you, you self-righteous prick." My fists balled up out of habit. It was no secret that the band dumped me after a few world tours. Apparently I was too much of a rock star for them to handle.

Inevitably, some drunken redneck would call me out at a bar and get put on his ass. What was so wrong with that?

"What's all this about us getting written *out* of the will?" I relaxed my hands. I wasn't going to pick a fight with him, not yet anyway, and definitely not here. Dad asked me to come home immediately, so I did. I only got the voice mail from the lawyer last night when I was drunk, and I managed to erase it by accident.

I was going into all this more or less blind.

"We don't start and stop at your request, little brother." He shoved the door open for me. "Go find out for yourself."

Fine by me.

I brushed past him and went inside. The sooner I could get out of here the better.

The scent of cleaners and hardwood filled my nose and triggered my nostalgia. I immediately thought of the one time I snuck Molly into the house when she was supposed to be at her friend's sleepover. That was well before we fooled around for the first time. We stayed up most of the night talking about the places we'd go together once we turned eighteen.

The butler told me that Dad had had the first floor reading room retrofitted into his new master bedroom. That struck me as odd. It was smaller than any of the actual first floor bedrooms and was the farthest away from the kitchen. I knew he was sick, but why he'd choose a room without a bathroom or even a closet was anyone's guess.

I ducked into each of the empty bedrooms I passed until I found a silk button down shirt in one of the closets.

It was a little tight, but it'd do fine. I didn't want to see my father looking like a complete scrub. Dad and I didn't always see eye to eye, but I respected the man and I knew he loved me.

I walked through the foyer, the kitchen, and the family room. The house hadn't changed much from how I remembered it. The ebony Steinway piano had the same high-gloss shine and was lit in a way that made the entertaining room glow. Mom desperately tried to get Richard and me to play, but we just weren't having it.

Molly played though. Holy hell could she play....

Whenever she came over, the whole family would stop whatever they were doing and listen to a few songs. I could still see her fingers gingerly wandering up and down those ivory keys like it was yesterday. I'd rarely ever seen my mother smile so brightly with pride.

Everyone loved Molly.

I shook the image from my head and forced myself from the room. I had to get out of there before the damn memories ate me alive.

"Ah, shit," I muttered under my breath, entering Dad's new bedroom.

It was the IV stand and the EKG machine I saw first; then I was hit with the scent of lemon pledge and a concoction of chemicals that I'd never be able to name. A nurse stood next to his new deluxe hospital-style bed and marked down his vitals on a clipboard.

All of the new sensory information smashed together, creating a gray sludge in my head. None of it made any sense. The room and the experience of coming home was more or less familiar, but completely alien at the same time. It was like when a character was suddenly replaced by a different actor on your favorite TV show.

I knew it was bad, but I didn't know it was *this* bad.

"Lucas, come on in." Dad was bare to the waist and looking tired. He usually kept a figure whose jolliness rivaled Santa Clause and now… well, he was thinner than I'd ever seen him, and it scared the hell out of me.

"Hey, Dad." I slowly stepped into the room, careful not to knock any wires loose. The nurse flashed me a respectful smile as she walked past, no doubt to give us a moment to ourselves. "How're you feeling?"

"With both hands." He smiled, slowly pushing himself off the bed. For being an industry giant, he was always surprisingly quick with a few bad Dad jokes. He put a shirt on, then clasped his hands over my shoulders and looked me over as if seeing me for the first time in a decade.

Dad and I weren't super close, but we still talked occasionally. After Mom died, we all stopped doing the holiday get-togethers. It was amazing how much she held the family together.

There was never any reason to come home anymore, but I'd still see Dad a few times a year whenever we both happened to be in the same cities. He'd usually take me out to dinner and tell me about some new breakthrough in medicine or technology his company was working on.

"How have your jokes gotten worse over the years, Dad?"

"Practice, my boy." He patted my shoulder. "If it's worth doing once, it's worth doing—"

"A thousand times." I smiled, cutting him off. He'd probably told me that around a thousand times too. It used to annoy the crap out of me, but this time I was glad to hear him say it. It made this whole experience feel more normal.

"It's good to see you, Lucas." He hugged me, and I hated how far my arms were able to wrap around him.

"You too, Dad." My voice broke off at the end. My eyes started to water like I'd been punched in the nose. Again.

Shit. I wasn't prepared for any of this. I thought I was coming back to hear that he was getting remarried or something. I should've known better. Mom was the only one for him. I'd never seen him with any other women after she died.

King men only ever fell in love once, and when we did, we fell hard.

The only exception to that was Richard. He'd never fallen in love, at least not to my knowledge. I wasn't even sure the corporate robot knew how to spell the word *love*.

We broke apart when the nurse came back in with a tray of steaming food. Dad made his way to the wall of windows, dragging the wheeled IV stand behind him like he was leading a child, then put a hand on the glass.

It was only then that I realized why it was this room instead of any of the others. From here he could see all of Caldwell Hope.

With his factories and his charity work, a lot of families depended on him. It was more than just that though; he put this place on the map and had the biggest hand in its growth. It was obvious that he cared a great deal about the people here.

He still thought of it as *his* city.

He was their protector.

"How bad is it?" I asked the nurse. She hesitated, drew in a deep breath, considered her words, then just frowned. Dad didn't bother to turn back around.

Jesus... my stomach twisted. I had spent so much of my life actively trying not to give a damn about anything, and all that training was undone in but a few moments of tense silence.

I was really worried.

Richard walked in a moment later. All the elitism and disapproval he'd thrown my way earlier was gone. There was only an uncharacteristic graveness in his features, which bordered on genuine sadness. Then he looked at me. "It's bad."

CHAPTER 4

Richard

"You've got to be kidding." I was as stunned as if I'd just grabbed a live electrical wire. "You want us to do what?"

I knew the terms would be… unconventional, but this was *insane*!

"You heard me." Dad was still facing out the glass door that led to the backyard. "The first of my sons to produce an heir will receive all of my assets and fortune. The other gets nothing. Not one red cent."

Dad turned back to us, stopping at Lucas first who was leaning against the wall near his bed. "Lucas, your fame has left you detached from people. You're incredibly talented, but also reckless. You need patience and something in which to be invested."

Then he walked over to me.

"Richard, your passion for industry and self-mastery

has allowed you to achieve more than I could've ever dreamed of, but it's come at the expense of everything else. You need to learn to step back and see the whole picture.

You both lack lasting personal connections, and you're too blinded by your own success to see how important that is."

"Dad." Lucas pushed himself off the wall. "I know I didn't turn out exactly how you wanted, but what you're asking is... it's fucking crazy."

I shot Lucas a sour look. He was our father not a construction worker at the dive bars he's used to playing at. "What he means is, leaving all of this up to chance isn't wise. There are so many things that could go wrong. This is a lot of money we're talking about."

"Five point two billion dollars to be exact," Dad said, as if the number was more of a burden than a blessing. It gave me pause. "Boys, I'm dying, and the only way this family survives is through children."

When you really boiled it down, money just meant options. How could billions of options ever be a bad thing?

"I don't like talking about this, but let's get it all out on the table," Lucas said. "What happened to the will you had while Mom was alive? Fifty-fifty split between your surviving heirs. That was fair."

"Fair?" What did Lucas know about fair? I was the one who went on to college, then grad school. *I worked my ass off to continue and grow the King legacy.* "Where have you been these last ten years? In no universe is getting high and plucking your guitar worth two billion dollars."

"You know what happened, Dick," Lucas growled. "I *had* to leave."

"Yes, I know why you left." I turned to give Lucas my undivided attention. I hated that damn nickname. He matched me with a scowl. Lucas leaving when he did was the only responsible and selfless thing he'd ever done. That didn't give him a free pass to act like an asshole the rest of his life. "But tell me again why you never came back?"

"You—" Lucas stepped toward me, his hands balled into fists.

"Boys," Dad interrupted.

"Now don't get me wrong," I continued anyway. *This was a long time coming.* If we were putting everything on the table, then this needed to be addressed as well. "I think Lucas is entitled to *something*, but half was always insane. We should use this time to consider a percentage more in line with his contribution to the King brand."

Which was zero, but I was willing to let him have something.

"Richard...," Dad said weakly.

"Dad, you've built an empire on rational, methodical decision making—"

"And that time has passed." Dad rapped his wedding ring against the glass window. The sharp sound split the air with authority.

I went silent and patiently waited for him to continue.

I had a tendency toward overtalking when I had a point to make, but that was because I was practically raised in a boardroom.

He turned back to us with a half-smile, then touched something on the doorframe, and the glass door beside it opened effortlessly. "Walk with me. It's too nice a day to spend cooped up inside the house."

It was too much money to be discussing with such an informal air. We were talking about *billions of dollars*. And what happened if he died before either of us got a woman pregnant? This was all such a bad idea. Lucas and I gave each other a wary look, then followed to either side of him. This might've been the only time we ever saw eye to eye on anything.

The back patio was antique blue marble that abutted an invisible-edge swimming pool. It wasn't all that wide but ran the length of the house. Beyond that was all of Caldwell Hope. It was probably the most expansive and gorgeous view in all of Colorado.

It was amazing that, as beautiful as this valley was, you only truly appreciated it when you didn't see it every day. We truly were spoiled kids.

"What's the difference between two billion dollars and five billion dollars?" Dad asked, walking over the short bridge that went over the pool. There was a small sitting area just on the other side that brought us to the end of the estate and the valley's edge.

"I don't know, Dad. The GDP gap between Greece and Kazakhstan?"

Lucas snorted behind me, incredulously. He tossed a pebble down the cliff that began a few dozen feet away. "Christ... he's obviously gearing up for a metaphor, Dick. Keep up."

"As always, you're both so right in all the wrong ways." Dad smiled, then sat down on the stone bench. "There is no difference. It's just a number. A man can't spend that money in one or even several lifetimes.

"When numbers control your life, it's easy to lose perspective, and in the end you wonder if it was all worth the cost."

"C'mon, Dad, you've done great things. Look." Lucas pointed down the valley at the bustling main drag of downtown. "I've seen pictures of this place in the fifties from before you moved here.

"The place was a shithole, a dying mining town. Now look at it. Tourism, industry, expansion, and urban development—it's all thriving. You've literally breathed life into Caldwell Hope!"

"I originally came here to meet with yet another potential investor. It was the first assignment my father ever gave me. 'To be your own man,' he told me, 'you have to able to make something out of nothing.'

"It was supposed to be the first step in building my own branch of King Industries." Dad squinted, but we were too far away to make out the individual building's signs.

I'd heard this story before. It was what he told me

when he sent me out into the world after I finished college.

"Long story short, no matter what I tried, the guy wasn't interested. I failed. I'd have left town and gone back east that very day if I hadn't met your mom. Maggie was my waitress. She wore this blue-dotted apron." Dad smiled warmly, remembering the way his wife looked when they met. "Here I was, looking miserable, and she brought me an ice cream sundae on the house."

This part I hadn't heard. It struck me that I never knew how my parents met. That seemed like something every child should intrinsically know.

"I didn't know you met Mom in a restaurant," I said.

"Yup, it was Cindy's Diner at the corner of Main and Marshall Long Avenue. It's long gone."

"It's a place called Black Rocket Records now." I chuckled quietly to myself in disbelief, thinking of the pretty and rude barista I'd met there this morning. I think Mom would've liked her, actually.

"We hit it off, and I decided to stay for a little while. She helped me through a real low point in my life. I was fresh out of college with almost two dozen failed attempts at finding investors already under my belt. It would've been impressive if it wasn't so damn disappointing." Dad wore a soft, light expression, finding the levity in even bad times.

"Your mother was the most incredible person I'd ever met. She loved good people and good books.

She lived her whole life in this small town. She never went to college, but she was such a smart cookie, and she loved children. That's why she spoiled you so damn much." Dad bent forward and lightly slapped our thighs.

"Anyways… I was about to abandon the idea of being an entrepreneur altogether and go back to my father with my tail between my legs and beg for a job. Maggie talked me out of it. When I told her what happened with the investor and my track record thus far, she said something I'll never forget.

"She said, 'So what?'"

He let that linger for a moment before continuing.

"It didn't matter that I failed. It wasn't the first or even the hundredth failure that mattered. It was the *last* failure that mattered, the one that stopped you from trying again."

"I get that." I crossed my arms, swishing the statement around in my mind like a fine wine. "Never give up, keep trying until you—"

"No, you don't." Dad put a hand on my shoulder. "Sometimes victory itself is a form of failure. You're too much like me to really understand."

Okay, now I was confused. The man was a self-made billionaire and philanthropist, how could being like him be a bad thing?

Lucas was strangely quiet. Did he actually know what Dad was talking about?

Sometimes it frustrated me that everything came

so easy to Lucas. I had to pour my blood, sweat, and tears into all that I'd achieved. Lucas was just naturally talented and floated through life like a breeze.

"The reason I've never told you that story before was because I was always too busy with work. I was too busy winning to see what I'd lost. Even after the empire was created, there was always more work to do, always more reasons not to enjoy what I already had. I might've never failed my business, but I certainly failed my family.

"Your mother especially…."

Mom cheated on him once when he was too busy to make time for her. It had been a dark moment in our family. The King family dealt with the quiet repercussions of that affair for years. In some ways, we were still dealing with it.

"I won't do that again," Dad said, somberly.

He was speaking of her spirit and how he would honor it. That part I got. The rest though…. How do you get defeated by constantly winning?

"You're right," I said. "I don't understand."

Dad sighed and stood up. "I've given this a great deal of thought. My decision is final and legally binding. I want a grandchild."

There was a long silence as he let that last statement sink in. All of this was so he could get a grandson or granddaughter?

"There are a few rules," he said. "No bribes in any capacity. You can't give a woman any money or incentives to do anything she normally wouldn't do."

"No paying for sex, Dick." Lucas stabbed the words at me like a knife between the ribs.

"Oh, please." *As if I would ever have to resort to that.*

Dad held up a hand to end our bickering.

"This town has some of the finest people in the world. You'll never find a better woman from anywhere else. The last stipulation is that my future grandchild's mother has to be from Caldwell Hope. Just like your mother was." Dad looked us over one final time, then walked back into the house, leaving Lucas and me on the bench overlooking the valley.

"There really is no way we're changing his mind on this," I said more to myself than to Lucas.

I had to *father a child.*

"Fucking crazy...," Lucas said in the same distant manner. He was still processing the information as well.

Years of problem solving clicked on like a light bulb. My brain started breaking down the challenges, organizing them, developing little plans to overcome each obstacle. Success was just a numbers game—trial and error. Exposure to the people and the area was my first hurdle. I'd been gone for so long. How was I going to meet a lot of eligible women in the shortest amount of time possible?

How could I get the most bangs for my buck?

Then it dawned on me.

Lucas looked over at me, apparently seeing that there was a big idea written on my face. "What are you going to do?"

What was *I* going to do?

I looked him dead in the eyes and said, "I'm going to win."

CHAPTER 5

"Are you *the* Lucky Luke?" A young blonde sidled up to me at the bar.

I fucking hated that stage name.

And after what happened with Molly a week ago, I certainly wasn't feeling all that *lucky*.

I had just started my night drinking in this hole-in-the-wall dive bar attached to a crappy motel on the outskirts of town. Only regulars, truckers, and those lost physically or mentally ever came here. I didn't think it even had a proper name.

I thought for sure I'd be able to drink in peace here.

"Nope." I gulped down the last of the beer I'd been nursing for the past half hour and slid a hundred under my glass for the bartender. Her comment made this one more drinking spot where I couldn't relax and be, so I got up and left the building. I wasn't even buzzed yet, and I was already running out of shady bars to drink at.

How else was I going to dull the thoughts that circled through my mind like vultures picking at a fresh kill. Soon I'd be stuck inside my hotel room drinking.

How pathetic was that?

I walked over to my bike, sat on the seat, and pulled a pack of cigarettes out of the breast pocket of my half-buttoned, black, linen shirt. Every time I sparked up, I reminded myself how terrible a habit it was. I wanted to quit, but never really had any reason to.

Considering what some of my other bandmates were hooked on, I'd say I got off easy.

Knock a girl up or lose my inheritance. That was fucking insane!

I couldn't shake the conversation we had earlier. It had been on my mind almost as much as thoughts of how bad I fucked up with Molly.

I loved my dad, but he must be losing his mind. I can't just slam a baby into some girl and be done with it. For all his faults, I didn't *think* Richard could either.

But what the fuck did I know?

Yeah, I slept around a lot when I was young, stupid and wrapped up in the rock and roll lifestyle, but I always used protection. *Always.* It wasn't just to keep my cock clean, but also so I wouldn't get a girl pregnant.

I actually loved kids; I just wasn't ready to be a father yet.

I knew myself better than to think I could raise one alone. They were a big deal! That's one of the things that made a guy into a *man*. The other was finding and protecting the woman you loved.

And just like that, I started thinking of Molly for the hundredth time today. I had a lot to atone for in our past, regardless of how much of it started out as my fault. The fact of the matter was that I wasn't there when she needed me, and that ate me alive every damn day.

After all this time, I come back home only to fuck up with her again! Money, fame, the satisfaction of beating Richard out of his inheritance... I'd give it all up for one more chance to do right by Molly.

I sucked in one last lungful of smoke, crushed the cigarette—still burning ember and all—in my fist, then started my bike. "Let's see what the next town has for bars."

I'd barely left the parking lot when I heard shouting. Fame had trained me to never turn around for shouts, it was just an opening for photographers to catch you in the worst light imaginable.

My bandmates never let me live down the tabloid cover photo that caught me looking up, midbite of shawarma with a headline that said something like, "Lucky Luke an Alien? Finally the Proof!"

It was pretty funny. They framed it and kept it in the studio while we recorded our last album together. God, that was years ago now....

No wonder, I thought, pulling out onto the main road. The shouts were coming from the parking lot of an MC clubhouse. *If nothing else, bikers knew how to make noise.*

I tried not to look; it was none of my business. Having a bike of my own was where our commonalities ended. But then I saw something that couldn't be ignored. The sun had only recently gone down, but exterior lights had already kicked on, allowing me to see the couple arguing in the parking lot.

I saw him—this tall, bearded, monster in a sleeveless leather vest—slap a woman to the ground and instinct took over.

In that moment, he could've been fifty feet tall and I still would've rushed him. I didn't care. You don't hit women.

Period.

The road was empty enough for me to stop where I was, put the kickstand down, and run toward them. I was no hero; I never went looking for trouble like this, but some things I just couldn't ignore. Mix that with an impulsive nature to begin with and, well... I made the news a lot.

Getting close, I jumped at the biker right as he turned to face me. One heavy right cross was all it took. He fell straight and slow like a large maple tree that had just been chopped down.

The knuckles in my right hand ached. *Fuck, that sonofabitch had a hard head.*

"Are you all right, miss?" I dropped to a knee and wrapped my good arm around the brunette to help her up.

"I think so," she said, picking up her glasses and letting me guide her to her feet.

Something on her wrist twinkled in the shitty parking lot light. A small, faded metal, heart pendant hung from her bracelet. My own heart skipped a beat and my breathing stopped being automatic.

"Molly?" I said in disbelief.

I gave her that for her seventeenth birthday. They were part of a matching set and had the word forever inscribed on the back. I swallowed hard to avoid choking on my own tongue. She was still wearing it....

Did that mean she still cared about me?

"Luke?" she said in hushed shout, then glanced around the parking lot. "What are you doing here?"

"I could ask you the same thing. The hell are you doing at a biker clubhouse? Are you out of your mind? And who the fuck is this prick?"

"OhmyGod, ohmyGod, ohmyGod," Molly panicked. "Do you have any idea what you just did?"

"Not nearly enough." A renewed rage washed over me when I looked down at the unconscious behemoth. Slapping a woman was bad enough, but hitting *my* woman… made me want to stomp his head in with my boots until my legs got tired.

How dare he touch her?

"That was the Black Chains *sergeant at arms.*" Molly began to push me back toward my bike. "You need to get out of here right now!"

"How bad could a biker gang based out of sleepy

little Caldwell Hope be?"

Molly lifted the back of the bikers vest, revealing a holstered pistol on the small of his back. Then she flashed me a hard look and said, "Bad enough."

She jolted away as the biker began to stir. He'd be awake soon.

"Please go, Luke." Her eyes pleaded with me. She was worried for my safety. She said she had moved on, but that wasn't the look you gave to someone you didn't care about.

She hadn't moved on. She still cared about me.

"I can't." My hand touched her cheek; it was red and hot from where he slapped her. I drew my lips in a tight line and looked at her firmly, unshakably. "Not without you."

A dangerous cocktail of emotions and panic flashed in her beautiful brown eyes. I wished I knew what was going on inside her head. There were so many things I wanted to tell her, but this wasn't the time or place for that.

She was right, soon other armed men would be on us. I only had the time to tell her one thing and I didn't even need words to say it.

I won't ever leave you again.

"Okay, fine. Let's go." She held out her hand. I grabbed it and led her toward my bike. "You can't take me home. That's the first place Cannonball will look. I need to go somewhere until he sobers up."

"Don't worry, I know a place that they'll never be able to follow us to." I helped her onto the back of the bike. "Cannonball? *Really?*"

"No one gets to pick their club names." Molly strapped on my helmet with an alarming amount of practiced skill. What was the story here? Molly was a librarian at an elementary school; what the hell was she doing hanging out with guys who had pirate nicknames? "And don't get any ideas. I still hate you for what you did."

"Yeah, I do too." I let out the clutch, kicked the bike into gear, and sped us out to the one place I knew she'd be safe.

It was also the one place I was *expressly forbidden* from going.

CHAPTER 6

Richard

"So, in closing, I thank you all for joining me tonight on my mother's birthday. This town meant the world to her. I'll leave you with a few words of wisdom my father once gave me when I asked him how I could best serve my friends, my peers, and my community. He said simply two words: *Open bar.*" I flashed my boardroom smile and waved through the thunderous laughter and applause.

I idly rubbed my cufflinks beneath the jacket of my two-tone midnight blue and black suit as I descended the stairs. It was a habit I had. Touching the cool silver always grounded me whenever I had to make speeches or big decisions.

The country club wasn't designed for presentations of this scale, so I had to retrofit their terraced flower gardens by the compound's main entrance with sound, lighting, and a stage.

My assistant and I made our way down to the sea of green between the valet and where the course proper started. The over five hundred initially assembled guests had started to disperse about the grounds, except for the journalists and reporters.

They *always* hung around.

I wouldn't have invited them if I had the option, but when it came to business and events, there was a certain way of doing things that was expected. They started in right away with forced pleasantries.

"What's your handicap, Richard?" one reporter asked.

"I don't golf."

"You bought the most prestigious golf club in the state for a party?"

"This might go down as the most expensive party in Colorado history."

"More of a celebration, really," I said. "Besides I've always wanted to try out one of those Segway golf carts they have here."

I answered their barrage of questions as quickly and efficiently as I could until it turned to updates on my father's decreasing health. At that point, I courteously bowed out and let my assistant, Jamie, give the canned replies and sound bites that they were all really after.

I spent the following hour meeting and talking with many of the guests. When I finally made it inside the building, I spotted my friends, Dempsey and his wife, Jillian, at the bar. They were a small safe haven where I could relax my public persona.

The night was far from over. It was a bad sign that I already needed a brief break.

"Impressive." Dempsey extended a hand with what looked like a Tom Collins cocktail. "You've managed to get all Caldwell Hope's single, attractive, and successful women in one place. I wish I'd thought of this when we were in college."

"Don't be rude, Lovebug." Jillian elbowed her husband for the joke, then stretched her arms to offer me a greeting hug. They had always been the greatest couple in my, albeit limited, group of friends. They flew in from California this morning to lend their support, and partly because they were bored and looking for something to do.

I quickly drained half the drink Dempsey gave me, not realizing how parched I was from talking so much.

"This was a lovely gesture, Richard." Jillian smiled warmly, then draped herself over her husband's shoulder. From her perfect blonde bun to the elegant way she moved in her six-inch heels, Jillian always had a regalness about her. She'd have been a queen had she been born in the right century and country.

"So who are you trying to impress?" She raised an eyebrow and settled in with a knowing smirk. She was also deceptively brilliant at getting to the heart of things. "Or are you trying to impress them all?"

"So you can say it?" Dempsey asked with some feigned indignation.

"Of course," she replied with a shrug.

"I'll have you both know, I carefully curated the guest list to include local artists, writers, bloggers, prominent cultural figureheads, and small business owners. I'm simply serving my community." I raised my glass for a toast.

Everything I said on that stage I meant. My mother did love this town, and I really liked the thought of honoring her birthday by bringing people together.

Meeting the best women from Caldwell Hope in one fell swoop was an added bonus. She would've wanted me to be happy.

And happiness to me meant beating my brother.

"Who was that golden-haired vision you were just speaking to?" Dempsey asked, swirling his nearly empty glass.

"That's Ms. Madison Grace, the governor's daughter." I kept glancing around the room as my friends and I talked. "Nice enough girl. I'll be taking her to dinner next week."

The night was still fairly young, and I'd already gotten the numbers or business cards of half a dozen beautiful young ladies.

That wasn't enough. I scanned the faces of the newest arrivals. Was I looking for someone?

I felt this odd sense of yearning. I was looking for someone else, someone *in particular*. I didn't know who that was until she was practically dragged into the room by her tall, blonde friend.

"If you'll excuse me…." I perked up at the sight of Gloria; the rude, yet vulgarly artistic coffee barista and co-owner of Black Rocket Records.

"Ah, yes," Jillian said. I could feel her smugly smiling as I walked away. "Go *serve* your community, Richard."

CHAPTER 7

Richard

It was immediately apparent as Gloria entered the grand room that she didn't want to be here at all. That only piqued my interest more.

Where Judy wore an elegant white dress and gold jewelry, Gloria was at the opposite end of the spectrum. She wore a black dress suit and shiny metal ear studs. The only exception in her outfit was a pair of bright red, low-heeled shoes that laced up the front.

You're not in Kansas anymore, Dorothy.

From her forced smile and body positioning behind her business partner—using her as a conversational shield—I could tell right away that Gloria wasn't shy or timid. This was a woman who had little patience for disingenuous niceties. Her little details were subtle, but telling, if you knew how to look.

I knew how to look.

Judy greeted me first; she was all smiles and saccharin. I braced myself for another tidal wave of words and general excitement as Judy delivered in spades.

"Mr. King, may I call you Richard? Thank you so much for your kind invitation! We're both extremely pleased to be here. We never got the pleasure of meeting your mother, but she sounds like such a wonderful woman. If you ever have any events that you'd like catered, we offer a coffee bar service. Oh, and that selfie we took got over five hundred likes on our Facebook page!"

I breathed in, smiling in exhaustion, and thanked them both for coming. I smoothly grabbed the arm of a passing food journalist and introduced—sacrificed—the man to Judy.

Stepping to the side of them as Judy began to talk to the journalist felt like suddenly being in a word vacuum.

That left Gloria and me relatively alone in a room full of people.

"Can I get you a drink?" I turned to Gloria. "It's only fair after that coffee you made me."

Gloria glanced back at Judy, who was laughing loudly in a small group of people. If they carpooled here, she wasn't leaving anytime soon. She turned back to me with a renewed fake smile. "Sure."

"You can drop the act and be miserable if you like.

I won't tell Judy, I promise," I said, walking toward the loneliest section of the room-wide bar I could find.

"What?" Gloria's fake smile cracked in surprise as I left her.

I briskly cut through small groups and politely pardoned myself before they could start up a conversation with me. I ducked under the bar, greeted the bartenders, and got to work making the most elaborate drink I knew.

The sparkling chandelier light wouldn't cut it, so I asked one of the bartenders to use the flashlight on his phone as I fished out ingredients under the bar. The mood lighting was nice, it made the hall more intimate, but I could tell it was difficult on the staff.

How could they work like this?

I took off my jacket, unbuttoned my cuffs, and rolled up my sleeves. Now that I owned the place, I was going to introduce a few changes.

"I'm not miserable," Gloria said, turning to get a better angle at what I was up to. There was a look of confusion and interest on her face. "Judy and I are both glad to be invited. There are a lot of people here that we wouldn't have been able to meet otherwise."

"Judy asked you to be on your best behavior, didn't she?" I began slicing papaya. I told the bartender what I was up to, and he assisted with the smaller fruits, gathering them from the kitchen and measuring them for blending.

"Mr. King—"

"Richard," I corrected, glancing up and momentarily getting lost in those stormy irises of hers. She really did have the most beautiful eyes....

"*Richard,* you don't know us well enough to make assumptions like that."

"But I'd like to." I stole another glance, this time with a half smile. "So much has changed since the last time I was here. I'd like to get reacquainted with my hometown. Would you be willing to show me around?"

"Absolutely not!" Gloria scoffed at the thought, then softened a little. "I'm sorry. I'm just too busy planning the record release party." She brushed a spiky black lock of hair from her sharp eyes. "Besides, I'm a terrible tour guide."

She seemed to have a habit of speaking her mind without a filter. There was a refreshing honesty to that, which I respected.

Gloria and I talked for a while as I wrapped up preparing the rest of the ingredients. I sent the various components off with the bartender to be blended, then washed and dried my hands.

"I've never seen a fruit salad with over fifty ingredients. I thought you were making drinks?" she said, trying to fill the void.

"I am." I smiled. The drink was called the Commonwealth, and it had seventy-one ingredients. "Like most things in life, it takes time and care to properly appreciate the simple beauty of complex things."

Gloria breathed in sharply as I met her eyes. She knew I wasn't talking about the drink.

"Why are you here?" I asked.

"We were invited," Gloria replied, getting a little defensive.

"You know that's not what I mean. I understand Judy—loud, fun, friendly. You, though...." I let the sentence linger while I mixed the juices and added the different alcohols.

"I'm only here to support the Rocket." She pursed her lips tightly. "That's it."

When the bartender returned I strained the drink, filled her glass and then decorated it with several mini flags and fruit slices. I slid the elaborate drink toward her from across the bar.

"How do I even...?" She raised an eyebrow at the glass, which was more of a piece of art than a mixed drink. I dropped a black straw in. "Ah, okay."

Gloria took a sip.

"Well?" I asked. I was proud of myself for pulling the Commonwealth off. The proportions were difficult to get right, and it took forever to make. I'd only made it a few times, and when I did it always impressed the woman I gave it to.

"Too sweet," Gloria said, after only the one sip, then slid it back to me. "Thanks, though."

"Really?" I deflated slightly. I tried it. It tasted fine.

I felt off slightly, like a machine that had stuttered through a gear set and hadn't properly synced back up yet.

"Yeah, sorry." Gloria leaned in and flipped over a clean rocks glass from the row that lined the inside lip of the bar, then reached for one of the bottles of whiskey I used. Stopping herself just before grabbing it, she asked, "May I?"

"By all means." I casually sipped at the monstrous mixed drink I made. I guess it was a *bit* sweet.

Gloria poured herself a shot, then downed it.

"What is it that you don't like about me?" I asked, curiously. It was a feeling I was unfamiliar with. This whole exchange was strange and interesting. Gloria definitely wasn't like the other women I met tonight. She certainly kept me on my toes.

I found that extremely attractive.

"I don't dislike you, Richard. We just don't operate on the same level. I'm sure you're probably a great guy to have tea with in *Milan* and—" Gloria flicked her eyes down my physique, trying to hide the swell of excitement in her gray eyes. "—a talented *polo* player."

"Polo?" I laughed, sliding the Commonwealth away and grabbing my own rocks glass. "Is that what you think I do?"

Gloria shrugged. "We *are* in an extremely expensive and exclusive country club, which you bought on a whim to throw a party."

I poured both of us a round of whiskey and turned my hands out. "Okay, that's fair. What you're saying is that you're not impressed by money. So tell me, what does impress you, Gloria?"

"I like music."

"Music, says the owner of a record store? Imagine my surprise." My sly grin stole away some of the firmness in her face. She was repressing a smile.

I, of course, took that as a challenge.

Right as I was about to follow that up with a joke, I noticed a certain uninvited someone walk in. "Goddammit."

"Everything all right?" Gloria cracked a surprised smirk at the abrupt change in my attitude, then followed my gaze.

My brother, Lucas, grabbed a few beers off a bar as he led a brunette through the room. I made a mental note to have a harsh discussion with the security guard that let my brother in when he was virtually the *only* person that *wasn't* allowed.

That wasn't just any brunette either. The glasses, the ponytail... she looked very familiar. Then it hit me like a ton of bricks.

Was that *Molly Baker?*

After what happened between them, I was genuinely surprised she didn't stab him on sight, let alone break into a party with him. She looked great, and despite the circumstances, it was really good to see her. For a time, when they were dating and she was always over at the house, Molly became like a kid sister to me.

Lucas searched the room with his eyes. When he found me, he smiled and winked. The gesture said, "You'll have to do much better than this stupid party to beat me."

Bastard!

"It's nothing." I said, forcing my expression to become lighter and more present. I refused to let Lucas destroy my night.

I shifted my attention back to the most interesting person in the room. It helped that Gloria's petite frame and tight curves were easy to lose myself in. "You don't like these sorts of parties, do you?"

"Being surrounded by people with their heads so firmly up their own ass that they could see what they had for lunch?" She blew out her air. "Not really, no."

"Why don't you leave then? Judy seems to have the networking angle covered."

"She's my ride." Gloria grimaced, shaking her head lightly. "She definitely did that on purpose, and I feel stupid for not seeing that coming. She is constantly trying to get me to meet people and be social, but I don't know. I guess I'm just not built that way."

"Let me give you a ride home then."

"What? No." She glanced back at Judy. Her partner's group had doubled in size, and she was the center of it. Judy laughed and flirted. It didn't look like she would be leaving in quite some time. The night was still young after all. "No, it's fine. Besides, this is *your* party. The host can't just leave."

"I doubt anyone would even notice." I scanned the room, seeing a wave of reporters enter the far end of the room. *Almost* anyone. "Either way, I'm tired of answering questions about my father's health."

Gloria followed my gaze and quietly understood my sudden desire to escape. There were so many things I could talk about for hours; my family and private thoughts were not among them.

"You're, of course, welcome to stay as long as you like, but I'm leaving." I texted Jamie to let her know I'd be stepping out for a while.

I draped my suit jacket across my arm—it had become too warm to put it back on— grabbed a bottle of top-shelf whiskey, then walked out from behind the bar. I reached for Gloria's hand to kiss it good night, but she clamped it tightly and shook it instead.

"It was a pleasure to meet you, Miss Grant," I said, amused. "Enjoy the rest of your night."

Judy's laugh split the air in the near distance and was followed by a round of rejoicing from those around her. Gloria's expression darkened. The thought of joining them or finding new conversations must have been really grating to her.

I felt surprisingly good as I walked away. Talking with Gloria for that brief time had been more satisfying than all the other girls combined. She had been a cool breeze in a room full of stuffy, stagnant conversations I'd already had a thousand times.

"Mr. King!" A deep voiced journalist ambushed me. "I'm with the *Caldwell Hope Journal*. Can I have a moment of your time please?"

"I'm sorry, I'm on my way out." Then a devious

idea hit me. I grabbed the man's shoulder and drew his attention toward Lucas. "But you see that guy over there with the long hair? The one person in this entire party who looks like he just stepped out of a music video?

"That's my rock star brother, Lucky Luke. He just told me that he wouldn't be getting back together with his band this time. They are officially done."

The man's dark face lit up at the thought of being the one to break the news. He thanked me profusely, then rushed off. A small crowd of other reporters could smell the fresh blood of a breaking story and followed the man. Within seconds, Lucas was surrounded.

I paused long enough to smile at his mounting frustration with all the questions, then turned to leave again.

"Wait," Gloria said, catching up to me as I made for a side exit. "Is that ride out of here still on the table?"

CHAPTER 8

Lucas

"Is it true that Gunmetal Tears is finally finished?"

"Did they kick you out after that stunt in Berlin? Are you going into rehab?"

"Care to comment on—"

I was up against the figurative wall, without so much as a final cigarette. Questions came at me like machine-gun fire.

I glared at Richard, but he was walking through the front door; a smile on his lips and the black-haired flavor of the night on his arm.

Shots fired, I thought, standing there as half a dozen reporters swarmed around Molly and me like vultures. I thought about the present I left in his car before coming in.

Enjoy the next few hours, Dick. After that, you're going to have a real bad night.

Their questions buzzed like bees, overlapping and interrupting each other as the reporters followed our escape from the grand room. They weren't particularly loud like in LA or New York; they were just relentless.

Molly covered her face, looking embarrassed. She wanted no part of this and definitely didn't want her picture taken. That flushed me with anger.

I had to get her out of here.

"Hey! No pictures." I loudly interrupted the stream of bullshit. "I'm not answering any of your stupid questions. Back the fuck off!"

I shoved my way through a small group of people as I led Molly to what looked like the server's egress that led to the kitchen.

"Hey! Jerk!" a tall, bubbly blonde in a white dress and gold jewelry shouted as I shouldered her out of the way. They picked the wrong set of swinging doors to hang out in front of.

At the last possible second, a fat photographer stepped in front of us and snapped a shot off. The white camera flash was blinding.

Instinct took over, and I latched onto the front of the camera. I'd have ripped it away from the photographer, but the lanyard was wrapped around the back of his neck.

"I said no pictures." I balled up my other fist and was about to take his head off when I felt Molly's hand tug at my cocked elbow.

"Don't be an idiot," Molly said. "Let's just go."

I turned and saw the whole room looking at me. Shit. I played right into Richard's hands. He *knew* this would happen. When I got riled up, I tended to act first and think later.

And nothing riled me up more than someone making Molly uncomfortable.

Well played, Dick. Once news of this got out, everyone in town would know I was back. That always made things more difficult.

The reporters followed us all the way to the staff kitchen before relenting. They'd have kept following us too, had the head chef not recognized what was going on and roared for them to leave. Fortunately the chef happened to be a fan and told us how to escape through the back by the dumpsters.

You'd think being a rock star would insulate you against the nasty back end of things, but that was never the case. I bet I passed more dumpsters in my career than any fan ever had. The public got the fancy front entrances with their gilded lights and flashy buy-me concessions and swag.

The artists got the back alleys and ugly hallways.

I didn't mind though. That's where I felt the most at home.

I glanced back at Molly when we made it outside behind the country club. Her bookish timidity had evaporated somewhere between me breaking into Richard's car and us sneaking into the party under different names.

I thought she'd be pissed, but there was a crease in the corner of her lips that someone might confuse with the ghost of a smile.

"It's amazing how little you've changed over the years," she said. "You're still an impulsive hothead."

Was she actually enjoying this?

It didn't matter that the gated-off staff area smelled like ripe trash or that I'd just made an ass out of myself in a room full of people. I couldn't remember a time recently where I was happier. Just being with her like this after so long gave the evening a magical quality.

What were the odds that I'd see her outside that bar at that exact time?

I never believed in fate or the shitty nickname I was given—*Lucky Luke.* I had no idea how all of this was going to shake out, but I was going to savor whatever time I could steal with Molly.

Even if she did still hate me.

"You've changed though." I shot her a quick glance, admiring the way her layered hair framed her perfect face. "When we were younger, it was a hell of a lot tougher to convince you to break into this place with me."

"I think I was afraid of disappointing your mom if we ever got caught." There was a gleam in her eyes as she shut the door and idly surveyed the endless green plane. The fog had started to conceal the distant tree line.

It was easy to forget the many good old times that

were buried beneath the mountain of bad times.

"Yeah, right. Mom would've let you get away with murder as long as you kept playing the piano. Do you still—"

"No," Molly said, curtly, obviously wanting to change the subject. She brushed a lock of hair back from her cheek and turned away.

I wanted to ask her why she stopped playing, but I held my tongue and pulled out a pack of smokes instead. I'd never seen anyone work the keys with half the finesse she had.

What happened to us?

It was a stupid question. I knew exactly what happened, and knowing didn't make it any better.

"Why'd you bring me here?" She leaned against the building's stone exterior and let her gaze slip up toward the heavens. Between the clubhouse, parking lot, and the various permanently lit driving greens, there was still too much light pollution to really take in the stars.

"Motorcycle vests don't generally meet the dress code here." I placed the cigarette in my mouth and flicked out a small flame from my Zippo. The yellow light highlighted the disapproval on Molly's face.

Smoking was so second nature that I hadn't even considered it might bother her.

"I knew you'd be safe here, at least for the night." I closed the metal lid on the lighter and killed the flame. Tucking the unlit cigarette away in my back pocket, I looked her over.

I didn't like the idea of her hanging around with men that hit women, but she declined when I wanted to get the cops involved.

Whatever was going on with her was a big deal, and it killed me not to know.

"What happened back there? Who the fuck was that guy?" I tried to keep the anger off my face, but I was still furious at that biker.

It was so hard not to get jealous too. When I heard that Molly had gotten married, I lost a week of my life to drugs, women, and bad decisions. I never fully recovered from the news.

"That's none of your business," Molly said, her lips were a tight slash across her face. Annoyed, she blew air out of her nose in a short burst, then looked away again. Right before she snapped her head to the side, I saw a glossy sheen in her eyes. "If you gave a damn, you'd never have abandoned me in the first place."

My heart lurched at the thought of being the one to bring tears to her eyes. I loved Molly more than life itself, but I never seemed to stop hurting her.

Fuck!

I stopped myself from punching the wall and busting my knuckles. I wanted to scream at the top of my lungs. This wasn't how any of this was supposed to go down! "Best laid plans are for idiots and assholes," Ricky, our drummer, was prone to saying when things didn't work out the way we wanted.

He was right.

I was both an *idiot* for thinking I could repair a decade worth of damage in one night and an *asshole* for jumping right in and trying. I was being selfish. I wanted my Molly back, the girl that loved me.

But that girl was gone.

"Listen," I said, ducking around in front of her and placing my head against the cool stone wall. "You're stuck here for a few hours until... whoever that was gives up looking for you.

"For the rest of the night, can we just be two different people?"

"Luke, it doesn't work like that." Molly bowed her head and lifted her glasses so she could wipe the tears from her eyes.

"I don't want to be Luke King," I said. "That dude fucked up so much that even *I* have trouble spending time with him."

I dropped to one knee so I could look up into her dark amber eyes. The gesture spurred an exasperated look to wash across her face. "Just for tonight." I pressed my hands together like I was praying to a god. In some ways, I was. "Just for tonight, let me be... Elmo."

"Elmo?" Molly snorted and shook her head, her face lightening. I was hoping for a smiling flash of her perfect teeth, but none came. "Like that lame plushy you won for me in that stupid claw machine?"

"There was nothing stupid about that claw machine. It was very good at separating idiots from their money." I spent over a hundred bucks over the course of a week trying to win that red, plastic-eyed jerk for Molly, all because she said it was cute as we walked by. She always had a thing for nostalgia. "What do you say?"

Molly sighed, walking away. The white blouse and jeans made her look like an angel that was slumming it for the weekend. She propped her hands on her hips and thought on it for several agonizing minutes.

"Fine." She turned back to me. The auxiliary lighting was dim enough for her freckles to have retired for the night, but the lenses of her glasses still shone defiantly. "On one condition."

"Name it," I said without hesitation, hopping back up to my feet.

"We might be stuck here, but I don't want to be anywhere in smelling distance of a dumpster."

The corner of my mouth spiked up, but I caught it before it got out of control and became a full-on grin.

I thought on it for a second. It'd been forever since the last time I was here. This golf course was massive, but most of it was empty for obvious reasons.

Where could we go?

I sure as hell wasn't going to take us back inside with all the reporters. There were a few smaller clubhouses spread out on the property, but those would all be locked up.

"There's a lake a ways down." A specific spot popped into my head, the way a long forgotten memory might when a song you hadn't heard in ages played on the radio.

Was *it* still there, I wondered?

The alarm reminder on my phone started buzzing. I turned the vibration off, but the text notification was still on the screen. It read: "Fuck with Richard? YES or NO?"

I thought about how Richard fed me to the wolves inside, and an evil smile spread across my face. I tapped YES, and it started auto-dialing.

I was willing to play nice, at least for a little while, but so much for that.

It looked like the King brothers were officially at war.

"What's so funny?" Molly asked, noticing my shark-toothed grin.

"I'm overwhelmed by brotherly love." I winked at her as the line picked up. "Hello, police? I'd like to report a crime."

CHAPTER 9

Richard

"This is me." Gloria collected her handbag as my Aston Martin slowed to a stop just outside Black Rocket Records. She thanked me for the ride, and I wished her a good night.

I certainly didn't want the night to end, but I wasn't leaving town any time soon—my father made sure of that—and I was willing to take it slow and figure her out.

Gloria Grant intrigued me.

She was a beautiful puzzle—a Rubik's Cube with razor-sharp edges and a mirror finish. I loved challenges, *lived* for them.

"Are you going inside, or are you headed back to your car?" I asked through the open passenger window when she closed the door.

"Why?" She gave me a distrustful look.

"It's late." It wasn't that late, but all the shops within eyesight were closed. "I'm going to stick around to make sure you get to wherever you're going safely."

As Caldwell Hope evolved into a tourist hot spot, more lights and late-night shops would eventually liven the place up in the evenings. It wasn't there yet, and without the perpetual bustle of people, the main drag looked lonely and unwelcoming. Violent crime wasn't a thing here, but it was dark out and if nothing else it was good manners to see her get to where she wanted to go. If I was being honest, I was also just looking for reasons to watch her go.

Gloria looked down, trying to hide her small smile.

"You're wearing the wrong suit to be a white knight," she said, looking back up at me. "I'm headed back into the shop for a bit." She paused, running something over in her head, then decided to continue. "You want a coffee? Y'know, as thanks for the ride."

"That depends…." I reached behind the passenger seat and pulled out the bottle of whiskey I stole from my new country club. "You mind if I bring my own sweetener?"

"Nope. If we had our liquor license, whiskey would be on the menu," Gloria said from over her shoulder as she walked to the door.

I got out and checked my key fob. I locked the car doors, unlocked them, then locked them again. The lights flashed and horn beeped obediently.

Everything seemed to be working fine.

Odd, I thought.

When we left the country club, my car doors were unlocked. I didn't have anything in there worth stealing, so it wasn't a big deal whether they were locked or not, especially not in a town with as low a crime rate as Caldwell Hope. Still, I specifically remembered locking the doors. The batteries in the fob must be dying.

Gloria unlocked the store, turned on the lights, and fired up one of her elaborate drip contraptions. As we waited for the coffee to percolate, she showed me around.

I hadn't noticed it the first time I came in here, but the shop had an excellent design to it. The layout of each section—records, unique and rare books, T-shirts, and coffee counter—flowed perfectly into each other without feeling cramped. The aesthetic was bold, thick swaths of color that gave the place an energetic and punk-rock feel.

A lot of care went into this place.

"Black Rocket Records is your baby, isn't it?"

"Every stain and bent nail." Gloria tried to downplay it, but I could see that she took pride in her work.

"You have some good stuff in here," I said, browsing through the racks of records. I slipped out an album by the New York Dolls. "Can I throw something on?"

"Sure." Gloria raised an eyebrow at my selection, genuinely surprised I picked something as fast, harsh, and dirty as the Dolls. She cocked her head to the side as she pulled out what could only be described as a beaker of coffee. "The iPod is behind the counter. It has all their albums on it."

That made sense. It'd be horribly impractical to be changing records over every half hour when working. Scrolling through her vast digital selection, I forwent the albums and just put it on shuffle. I knew a little of the punk-rock genre from when I played bass with Lucas as kids, but not enough to hold any kind of conversation about individual bands.

The thrashing punk song ended and something a little bluesier began.

It wasn't always bad between Lucas and me, but I tried not to think about those days. It was easier that way.

"Hey, spaceman." Gloria roused me from thoughts of my past, a wary look in her eyes. *What kind of problems could a billionaire possibly have?*

I might not have had to worry about my mortgage or debt, but I did have to fall in love and have a kid or else I'd lose my entire inheritance. It sounded like a cautionary tale that you'd find in one of those old Brothers Grimm-style fairy-tale books.

Not the Disney ones with the happy endings.

Gloria placed the steaming mugs of coffee down by the register on the glass countertop that had all the Alice in Wonderland art. I grabbed the whiskey on my way over to her.

"You wanna do the honors?" she asked, waving a hand toward the booze.

"I don't want to mess up whatever magic you've got going on in here, but I'll be your assistant." I unscrewed the top and slid the bottle to her; then I grabbed a stool from the long seating bar at the window and sat opposite her on the customer end of the counter. "Déjà vu."

"Yeah, sorry about that morning...." Gloria scrunched her mouth to one side, looking mildly guilty. "I didn't mean to snap at you last time. I had just gotten into an argument with Judy and was in a pissed-off mood. I'd like to think I'm not usually *that* rude."

"You're just lucky the coffee was phenomenal." I winked at her, then let myself relax enough to relate to her on an honest level. "I get it. We all have bad days."

"What should we toast to?" She poured and mixed the drinks, then held hers up.

"To the Rocket's massive revenue growth this quarter."

"Jesus, man." Gloria chuckled, sinking into a stool she had on her side of the counter. "No. I mean, yeah, I hope we do well, but that's not something you toast to."

"No?" I thought back to my last several business dinners. "That's all my shareholders seem to care about."

"No! You toast to health and good tidings. Vague things that make you feel happy even if you know they're lies."

"Okay...." I blew the steam off my coffee as I thought it over. Raising my cup again, I gave it another try. "Here's to new, *unlikely* friends. Better?"

"Better." Gloria's black-rimmed eyes softened, and a hint of a smile creased her lips on one side. I hadn't figured out if they were contacts yet. They *had* to be. I'd never seen a stormy shade of gray like hers before.

It was easy, *too easy*, to lose myself in them....

My father's challenge softly echoed in my head as we locked stares.

I abruptly broke my gaze, sipped my coffee, and surveyed the room. A wave of shame slithered up my spine.

Damn. I hadn't even slept with this girl and that's what floats across my mind—*How can I knock her up and win the competition?*

I'd been with so many women that it was hard to remember them all. Through it all, I'd always been up front and honest about my intentions and my commitment level, or rather *lack of* commitment level.

I showed them all a fun, hot time and never had any regrets. It was just sex.

So why did I feel so sleazy now?

I didn't like it. I was known to be ruthless, cold, and maybe a bit of a jerk, but never dishonest. I had to get the truth out of the way now.

"I never wanted to come back to Caldwell Hope," I said a few minutes later, finishing my coffee. The blues song faded into something by Buddy Holly.

She finished hers and poured herself a two-finger refill of just the whiskey. "And yet here you are." Then without asking, she poured me a refill too.

"Are you trying to get me drunk?"

"It's bad form to let a lady drink by herself. Besides, you're a big guy, you can handle it." Gloria shrugged and smiled. Her demeanor had softened so much since I met her.

Had I broken through her prickly armor? I doubted it, but she had at least lowered her sword from my throat.

"So why did you come back?" she asked, looking me over again. I noticed her inspection was a lot slower this time. Her eyes took their time over my muscles and down to the bunched fabric that protected the world from my cock.

"I'm only here because of my father."

"I heard." Her face tensed with genuine concern. She sipped at her drink with tentative discomfort. She didn't need to know me to understand having a parent slowly dying was terrible. "I'm sorry."

"It's not just that." I knocked back the rest of my whiskey and poured more. "I'm here because in order to *win* my inheritance, I need to get a woman pregnant before my brother does."

"Jesus." Gloria leaned away from the bar, her face screwed up. "Is that why you drove me back? Are you hoping to impregnate me to win your contest?"

"No." I laughed. "*Of course not*. Not even I'm

that callous. If I was and that was the goal, I wouldn't have been honest with you."

"Why the hell should I believe you?"

"I'm a lot of things—" I looked up at her with nothing but naked sincerity on my face. "—but I'm no liar."

Gloria darted her gaze away, and I felt a pit form in my stomach. I wanted her to believe me.

Why was that suddenly so important?

I barely knew this girl, and there was no way she'd be the woman to have my kid. I was just wasting my valuable time with her when I should've taken some other girl home—some rich, dull blonde that would be receptive to the idea of faking a relationship long enough to give me an heir.

I knew all of that analytically, yet... here I was.

Gloria absently swished the last sip of whiskey around the bottom of the mug, finally swallowing it. After a refill and several more minutes of thoughtful introspection, she asked, "Why not just buy a hooker or something?"

"That's against the rules." I shrugged. I'd never had to before, and the thought hadn't even crossed my mind. I could just disregard the rules and pay someone to have my kid and lie about it, but that wasn't me. I wanted to win. *Really win.* "It also feels... wrong. I've never had to buy one before. I wasn't about to start now."

"Oh, there are rules?" She raised an eyebrow skeptically.

"I guess so. My father was very thorough when he wrote up all this insanity."

"I have no intention of getting pregnant," Gloria blurted unexpectedly. "Not for a long while."

Was she actually thinking about it?

I dismissed the thought. All the alcohol she packed into that tiny frame must have started to catch up with her; I hoped she wasn't driving anywhere soon.

"Besides, you already have a baby." I gestured in a wide arc about the store. In some respects, having your own small business was like having a child. You constantly have to feed it and help it grow or else bad things happened.

"All right, Mr. Bigshot." Gloria's eyes narrowed, but she leaned back in from across the counter. Her black, tussled hair fell in front of one of her eyes. Instinctively, I moved to brush it back, but fortunately I was still sober enough to stop myself. "It's my turn to ask you. What are you doing here?"

That was a good question. I was still trying to work that out for myself.

Gloria was unique in many ways. She was forward, abrasive, filter-less, and she generally didn't seem to care how people saw her. There was bravery to that, a boldness I couldn't ignore.

"I brought you back because you're more interesting to me than anyone else at that party." I brushed my thumb across her knuckles. "I know there's no future for us. You're not going to have my kid, nor would I even ask you to. But I'd much rather spend the night drinking with you than people with *'their heads up their asses.'*"

It was a weird truth, but truth nonetheless. Maybe I just needed a break from my life for a while. Maybe that's all Gloria was—a beautiful punk-rock pause button, a commercial break, a lungful of fresh air in a smoky hall.

Whatever she was, I knew I wanted it.

And from the way her lips cracked apart in a hesitant smile, I could tell she wanted the same. Her dark eyes were heavy, but it wasn't from alcohol or tiredness. I'd seen lusty eyes enough to know them right away.

Then her damn phone went off.

We both glanced at the time. One in the morning already? When someone calls this late, it's usually important. Gloria exhaled, letting her head dip out of exasperation, then roughly snatched her purse from beside the register. She fished her phone out and sighed again when she saw it was her partner.

I couldn't make out what Judy was saying over the music, but from her excited tone, I could tell that it was at least good news. What followed next was fifteen minutes of Gloria getting out half sentences before being cut off. She said *uh-huh* during that time more than I'd heard all week.

It struck me as odd that a woman like Gloria would tolerate this kind of partnership.

I'd learned in business that it was crucial to surround

yourself with different and occasionally contrasting points of view. It helped you look at problems from more than one way.

These two though... they were fundamental opposites.

"Tell me," I said when Gloria slapped the phone down and shoved it away from her like it was a napkin she'd just used to kill a spider. "How does someone like her become partners with someone like you?"

"She came with the money." Realizing how bad that sounded, Gloria clarified. "I didn't mean it like that. Judy is... well, her heart is in the right place. We went to high school together. I had the passion and the degree, just not the credit for a bank loan."

"But she could fund you." Things started falling into place in my head.

"No, but her father could. The caveat was that Judy be co-owner so she could get some real-world experience. She's great at being social, but still has a long way to go on a lot of other things." Gloria propped herself up on the counter so she could sit a little more comfortably. In doing so, her hand slipped and knocked her mug directly into my lap. "Dammit!"

I snatched the mug up before it could smash against the floor, but my pants weren't saved from a good splashing. Gloria shot up, looking horrified, then sprang off to grab a fistful of napkins from the dispenser.

"It's fine. It's only pants." Granted, they were expensive pants, but nothing I couldn't live without.

"When you say a long way to go, how do you mean?"

"She tied up all of our liquid assets in booking The Deconstructed to play here when their album drops."

"I've heard of them," I said slyly, playing it cool. I'd actually been a big fan back in the day. There was a time in middle school when Lucas and I learned a few songs, but we couldn't keep it together long enough to make the talent show.

It was a very short-lived idea.

"Yeah, they're a big deal. For what we're paying them, you'd think we're booking *The Beatles!*" Gloria's face brightened with repressed irritation as she continued to speak. The flush on her creamy skin could've lit up a small closet. "In theory, it'll be the biggest draw we've ever had, which should translate into a lot of sales, but if literally *anything* goes wrong...."

"I can see why you're worried. Rock stars aren't known for being reliable." Especially not that band. The Deconstructed practically had their own wing at a rehab resort in Florida.

"I probably shouldn't be telling you any of this." She paused, looking a little flustered. How long had she been holding this in for? She didn't seem to be the kind of girl that made friends easily.

For as different as we were, we did have a few things in common. I often compartmentalized my emotions so I wouldn't have to deal with them. It was great for efficiency and levelheaded decision-making, which was paramount when running a multimillion dollar corporation or a small coffee shop.

It wasn't so good for… anything else really.

"Your secret's safe with me," I said.

"Safe? I don't even know you." Gloria patted her forehead with the back of her hand. "Shit, am I blushing? I think I drank too much."

I rose off my little stool so I could easily reach her, then touched her face. Her cheeks were scalding like spilled coffee. She didn't pull away, so neither did I.

"You wear pink really well." I smiled. "You're like my own personal Lite-Brite."

"*How old are you*?" she teased playfully.

"Funny," I said, brushing the insult off. Thirty-one wasn't *that old*.

Her deep crimson lips curled up at the edges. At that moment, I wasn't thinking about my countless responsibilities at work or my father's illness or even beating Lucas for the inheritance.

All I wanted in life was to taste Gloria's sweet, pomegranate smile.

My hand shifted to under her chin, raising it slightly so her face was all I could see.

Over the store's speakers, the driving drums and crashing guitars of The Cure's song "Burn" thundered its dark melody just for us.

The paleness of Gloria's skin warmed in the subtle glow of the low-hanging yellow lights above us.

And her eyes....

Her eyes glistened like a storming sea, wild and

dangerous with sharp rocks lying just beneath the surface. I leaned into her, feeling like the captain of a doomed ship being lulled closer by a siren's irresistible song. Every bone in my body hummed, warning me that nothing good was going to come of this.

For the first time in my life, I ignored my instincts.

I kissed her.

CHAPTER 10

Richard

My tongue searched hers, discovering notes of coffee, black cherry, and hot whiskey.

It was better than I could've imagined.

Gloria was just over five feet tall; I had almost a foot and a half on her. She had to kneel on her stool and practically lay over the counter just to reach me. Had we been thinking straight, we'd have walked a few feet in either direction and not had a counter between us.

But the alcohol and lustful stares had pushed us far past the point of rational thought. Instead, I placed my hands at her waist and lifted her over the counter like she was a stuffed bear I'd just won at a carnival.

She was so light that I might decide to never put her down.

She wrapped her legs around my waist when

we were clear of the register and there was nothing between us but air and longing. I pulled her into me. Her heels slipped off, one then the other.

"Your ruby slippers, Dorothy...," I murmured distractedly between kisses. "You'll never get home now."

Gloria shrugged off the black suit jacket she was still wearing and said nothing.

I sat her on the counter and tore off my neatly tailored button-down. She tugged the bottom hem of my undershirt out from my pants and dipped her cool fingertips beneath the fabric.

"I've never met a desk jockey with abs before." Her hands gingerly slid up my washboard stomach and broad, sculpted chest as she finally rolled my undershirt over my head.

"It must be all that *polo* you think I play." I wasn't as gentle. In a flash, I had her tank top on the floor and her deep purple bra draped across the register. She sat before me, naked save for her pants and a devious smile that asked, *What are you waiting for?*

I paused to take in her soft alabaster beauty.

Hot ripples coursed down my body, pulsing directly into my hardening cock. Of all the women I'd been with, none of them looked like her. Gloria was sexy and exciting in a way that was so new.

Her skin was spun silk, and although there was faint definition in her ribs, she looked healthy and vibrant. Staring at her, drinking her in with my eyes, made her face flush a deeper shade than her dusted rose-breath areolas.

"You aren't like most people I know." She looked at me curiously, probably wondering why I was taking my time.

Why would I rush?

We had all night. Besides, any decadent dessert that you weren't likely to ever have again was worth savoring, wasn't it?

"Know many billionaires?" I dragged my fingers down her neck and palmed her modest chest. Closing my eyes, I felt her heartbeat pound softly against my hand. When I opened them again, I found her peeling back two of my fingers and tracing them with her tongue.

The ripple down my core became a scorching flood when she wrapped her mouth around my fingers and began to suck. Every swish of her tongue made tiny promises of what she could do when she was on her knees in front of me. My rock-hard cock threatened to bust through my fly. Her teeth clamped down, biting notes of pain into my flesh.

It made my breath spike.

"That's not what I mean," she said, licking the tips one final time before releasing me. There was vulnerability in her voice that genuinely surprised me. "Most guys I've been with barely even noticed me."

Here I was thinking this girl was all cactus and barbwire, but that really wasn't the case at all. I guess the honest things about a person were easy to overlook if you weren't searching for them. After all, most people thought I was just some spoiled, heartless corporate exec looking to fuck everyone over for the sake of a few more bucks.

When I met Gloria, she didn't even try to hide her judgmental disdain. Now though... she wasn't looking at me that way.

It was a really nice feeling.

With my hand still firmly planted on her chest, I gently pushed her down on the thick glass-topped counter. Her lithe, half-naked form squeaked when I dragged her hips closer to me. It wasn't that wide a counter; I didn't want her head hanging off the other side. Gloria blanketed most of the Alice in Wonderland collage, and I had to wonder…

Are we both falling down a rabbit hole of our own?

"You're all I see, Gloria." I lowered my mouth to her stomach as I said the words so she could feel the vibration through her skin.

Gloria breathed deep, and the tenseness in her muscles evaporated. Soon she'd go back to stressing about work, and I'd start interviewing the women I'd met at the party. But that was tomorrow.

Tonight was all ours.

She shivered as my fingers flicked over her nipples; they were as hard as setting clay. When I pinched them, she let out a little chirp and her smile widened wickedly. That was exactly how I liked it. Slow, mounting pressure.

It made the release that much more.

I kissed down her stomach as I unclasped her pants. Her body tasted delicious, like lightly salted shea butter with hints of flowers. Lipstick, makeup, perfume... she might not have wanted to be at the party earlier, but her body did.

I smiled, kissing over her hip, taking in her intoxicating natural scent. Her panties were plain cotton, but were a bikini style. I bet while she was working she was more of a boy-shorts girl.

Who was she hoping to see tonight?

I couldn't help but fantasize that she did all this for me. It was vain, but thinking that she was dolled up for someone else filled me with a strange jealousy.

Gloria moaned softly as I hooked the elastic band and jerked the thin fabric past her knees. Her pants hung lazily off one foot until she kicked everything off. My head was swimming as a carnal urge washed over me, and I grabbed her thighs roughly.

The back of her knees bent over my shoulders, and I dived in like a treasure hunter. I didn't hesitate; I couldn't if I wanted to. I was magnetically drawn to her smoothly shaved pussy.

I parted her pink lips and drank deeply, my tongue exploring every sensitive nook and fold. Her whole body jerked forward when I grazed her clit with my teeth. I watched as Gloria propped herself up onto her elbows, her eyes widened in fear and thrill.

"Fuck," Gloria moaned and writhed, causing more

chirp-like squeals from her skin sliding on the glass.

I had her now. *She was fully mine.*

My tongue was buried inside her, curling as far as I could go. There was nothing she could do except riffle her fingers through my hair, hang on, and pray. Sucking and stroking her clit, I realized that I was moaning too.

My cock throbbed.

Shit, I hadn't been this horny since I was sixteen. The more I tasted her, the more I wanted. I wanted to ruin this girl, make it so that every time she sat down she remembered my hard cock impossibly deep inside of her.

Gloria's body tensed so much that she was sitting fully up on the counter and was leaning over me. Her shock of black hair blotted out the overhead light. Suddenly she cried out and came.

I didn't stop.

Her pussy fought back, desperately trying to crush my tongue. I wasn't having any of it. I pried her thighs apart and pressed my face in harder. I could feel another orgasm on the wings screaming for me to release it.

Seconds later she came again, more violently this time. I had to catch her or else she'd have fallen off the counter.

"Fuck me already!" She squirmed, her body quivering from aftershocks.

Just as I was about to tear my mouth off her to reply, there was a sharp rapping on the Rocket's glass door.

"Shit!" Gloria's face went from beet red to ashen

white in a heartbeat. She swung backward over the counter like a drunken gymnast, knocking over a rack of gift cards in the process.

"What…?" I shot up to catch her, but I was too late. After I peered over the side to see that she was all right, I turned toward the door.

Two uniformed police officers stood outside, plain as day. They both looked down, embarrassed and amused. One of the men cautioned a glance up and knocked again.

"Coming!" Gloria cursed, then corrected herself, "I mean, *on my way!*"

How long were they standing there?

I put my shirt back on and discretely positioned my cock so that I wasn't tenting my pants. It was a straight, clear view of outside. They must've seen *everything*.

It's amazing what you don't think of in the heat of passion and when you're buzzed.

Having assembled most of her clothes, Gloria rushed over to the door and opened it. "Evening, officers. Is, uh...." Gloria cleared her throat. "What seems to be the problem?"

You mean aside from being eaten out in view of anyone walking by? I thought.

To our defense, it was late and the street was long dead. No one had even driven by since we'd been here. Black Rocket Records was on a corner so we'd have seen headlights flash if any cars were in the area.

Did someone walk by and call the cops?

That being said we obviously didn't see the cops pull up either so who the hell knows... To say we were distracted would've been underselling it. Fuck yoga and meditation. Having my face buried between Gloria's thighs was now my new favorite way of shutting out the rest of the world.

"Whose car is this out front here?" one of the men asked politely.

"That's mine." I did up the few remaining buttons on my shirt and walked over. There was probably a parking ban in effect. I hadn't been back long enough to catch up on the town's ins and outs. "Do I need to move it?"

"No, sir." The pleasantness hadn't left the lead officer's voice, but I did notice he was now resting his hand on his gun. *Never a good sign.* "But we do need you to unlock your vehicle. We need to search it."

"What? Why?"

"We received an anonymous tip saying you had well over the legal limit of marijuana in your trunk."

The news slapped me like a wet fish across the face. That was impossible. I didn't smoke weed. Then I remember my car was unlocked when I drove Gloria back from the party. All the pieces fell into place. I suddenly knew exactly why the cops were here.

Lucas.

CHAPTER 11

Lucas

Molly and I walked for hours. In the dark—our path lit by only moonlight or occasionally by cell phone when we strayed off the course and into the woods—we were seventeen-year-old kids again.

It was crazy how *easy* it was to slip back into that role. We were best friends before we started dating.

We talked about music and movies. She caught me up on Caldwell Hope politics and the aggressive tourism movement that had squeezed almost all the charm out of our small town.

She thought the new ski resort—that doubled as an adventure park in the summer months—brought too many rich, yuppie assholes into the area. What kind of example was that setting for the kids?

We mostly avoided the hard stuff—why I left and

what she was doing with bikers to begin with. The real world threatened to crash down around us like a driving rainstorm, but as long as we kept up our umbrella of light and hopeful conversation, it couldn't touch us.

I wondered how long we could keep it up before one of us finally cracked and demanded answers. I doubted it would be long. The thought of that biker slapping her made my knuckles itch.

She did most of the talking right up to when we arrived at the tucked-away lake, but I didn't mind. I'd forgotten how much I loved the sound of her golden-honey voice. I could listen to her forever.

It had always been like that though.

We walked along the bank, listening to the cicadas and the wind. The temperature had dropped just enough to be borderline chilly. She was only wearing jeans and a blouse. I noticed her spine ripple with a chill, and I cursed myself for not bringing my leather jacket to drape over her.

"Does Lucky Luke have any shows lined up now that he's back?"

"One, yeah. Over at the Family Room this Friday. Why?" I asked slyly. "You interested in going?"

"Maybe." She tossed me a tattered half smile. She was trying her best to keep up with our game of being different people, but we both kept slipping up. It was a nice fantasy though. I really liked the idea of a fresh start with her.

"You should go. I know the guitarist is a total

douche, but I hear he knows how to play."

Molly laughed, then looked around. "I think I remember this place."

"You used to read to me out here, you remember?" It was one of my favorite things in the world. I stepped behind her and rubbed some warmth into her arms. The shampoo of her soft brown hair filled me with nostalgia.

Whenever some blogger would ask me about inspiration for my songs, I'd tell them the same story. "A good story, a soothing voice, and the kiss of warm afternoon sun was all I needed."

It wasn't the full truth, but that was the point. The *real* truth was private. It belonged only to Molly and me. It was a precious memory that would lose some of its magic if I ever told anyone about it.

"I do," Molly said wistfully, looking out at the black, shining lake. The moon had slipped out from behind a cloud, generously lighting her face for me. The cool tones made her skin look as smooth as porcelain.

For a second, I worried that this was all a dream. Nothing was ever this perfect.

"You'd sit in the shade of one of those trees." I pointed up past the stump of a tree that'd been struck by lightning long before our time. "I'd lay my head on your lap, close my eyes, and listen to stories by Emily Brontë and Jane Eyre."

"Jane Eyre wasn't an author," she chided me like the librarian she was. "It was the name of a book by

Charlotte Brontë, Emily's sister."

I shrugged. I wasn't much for books in general. Maybe she ruined them for me. The voice in my head could never compare with the sound of her reading to me.

"Half the time, I thought you were asleep," Molly continued, breaking away from me and the bank and making her way up to the stump. She sat down.

"But you kept reading." I began searching the bark on trees I passed, but I couldn't find what I was looking for. God, it had been so long. It probably wasn't here anymore.

There was no way....

"I thought you might be able to hear me in your dreams." Her voice became a near whisper as she finished the sentence.

Her words stopped me dead in my tracks. My resolve began to crack. I looked back at her, trying to keep it together. There was a tidal wave of emotion washing over me. If only she knew how much I thought about her.

"You were right." *I heard you in my dreams for ten agonizingly long years.*

The pressure on my heart and soul had been building since the moment I first saw her again. She still wore my bracelet, even now. That had to mean something, right?

"Are you still married?" I winced as the words came out, but I had to know.

I shouldn't have brought her back here. This was all too goddamn painful.

What the fuck was I thinking?

"What happened to Elmo?" Molly looked at me warily. She was definitely trying to stay out of the hard rain that was about to fall, shielded safely under her umbrella of fantasy. If we didn't talk about any of it, then we wouldn't be soaked to our bones with guilt and regret.

"Fuck Elmo," I replied, harsher than I wanted. That pressure inside me boiled over. I thought I could pretend, but with her so close I couldn't bare it any longer.

I watched her face drop as I shattered the fantasy that we were just old friends out for a walk down memory lane. Molly crossed her arms and turned her back to me.

Dammit!

How did Richard do it?

How could he put his emotions in a box like a fucking robot while I always wore mine on my sleeve? That was the only thing he had that I was envious of, the ability to not be passionate.

All passion ever did was hurt the ones I loved.

"I'm sorry. I'm a fucking mess, Moll."

"No." Molly snapped back around, her voice taking on a ragged edge to it. She was suppressing an urge to cry. "You don't get to just ride in here and fuck with my life because you're a mess. That's bullshit!"

"One for one?" I took a few steps closer. One for one was a game we used to play. We did it when we were young and shy about what we wanted. I asked a question, then she'd ask a question, or vice versa. It was basically truth or dare without the dare.

It's how I found out she was terrified of albino cats and how she found out I hated the sound of damp fingers down the side of an inflated balloon. As we grew into two horny teens, one for one got a hell of a lot steamier.

Now as adults the game was going to change again. It would never be enough, but maybe knowing one thing about the other person might help a little.

Molly's puffy pink lips pressed together in a tight line as she considered it. Even behind her glasses, I could see the ache in her eyes. She wanted everything to be like it was between us but knew that was just a dream.

"Do you have any idea how long I waited for you?" Molly threw her hands up. "I waited and waited and fucking waited! Not a word from you until now?"

"I'm a bastard."

"You're goddamn right, you're—"

"No, Molly. A *bastard*." I ran a hand over my head, brushing my chin-length hair out of my face. "My perfect mother had a one-night stand with some musician from Tennessee during a real low point in my parents' marriage." I spread my arms out. "And I'm the result."

"What? No...." Molly stopped and gaped, not knowing what to really do with that bombshell. Eventually, she filled the silence by saying, "I'm sorry to hear that. What does that mean exactly? You're not a King?"

"Not biologically, no. Will, Richard's dad, adopted me when he found out about the whole thing. I guess they were able to keep everything quiet, but it was messy. *Real* messy."

Molly wrapped herself tightly with her arms and stayed quiet for far too long. "Is that why you left me?"

"I didn't know I was adopted until I was seventeen. I found out in the car ride over to the airport." I paused. I'd never told anyone this story before. It was hard to hear the words out loud. "I never wanted to leave you, Moll. I had no real choice."

"Jesus.... By who?" She sounded horrified.

"One for one." It was my turn to ask a question. Besides, I'd already said too much. She could do so much damage to my family with the information I just told her. "Are you still married?"

Molly sighed heavily. "Yes."

I slumped against a tree, idly rubbing my hand against the rough bark. What was I hoping for?

Finally, my fingers brushed across something cool and smooth. I snapped my eyes down and confirmed that it was what I was looking for. I crouched down and cleared away the brush.

Holy shit! It was still here!

"Moll, you have to see this." I pulled out my phone's light and lit the side of the tree.

Molly walked over slowly, a cautious interest in her dark eyes. What on a tree could possibly be so interesting? Some sort of carving maybe?

"When it was time for me to leave Caldwell Hope, I wasn't allowed to bring anything identifiable. I had no idea what was going to happen to me, so I took the only thing that ever mattered to me and I hid it out here."

It took a good amount of effort, but I was eventually able to wriggle the charm free. The branch that held the bracelet had grown in the years I was away and stretched out the bracelet. It was too big for even my wrist, but that was fine. I only cared about the heart pendent.

I grabbed her wrist, and my thumb rubbed across the bracelet charm I'd given her so long ago. Her skin was butter silk and made my fingertips tremble. She didn't pull away.

"I was going to come back for it, but then I heard you were married, and the thought of seeing it again was too painful." It was difficult, but I forced myself to look up at her. Her glasses shined brilliantly in the moonlight and made her eyes agonizingly unreadable.

"I'm... I'm trying to get a divorce," Molly said, reluctantly. "I was trying to convince Jason to sign the paperwork, but... well, you saw how that went earlier tonight."

"That was your husband!" I was now even more furious with that biker scumbag. I should've stayed and put that motherfucker in the hospital!

A husband should protect their wife, not hurt them.

"There were good times too." She turned, and the light refracted away so that I could see her eyes. They were full to the brim with tears that were just waiting to fall. It made me feel horrible for shouting at her.

"I'm sorry." I stood up and thumbed the first rolling tear off her cheek. "You deserve better, that's all."

"That was the only time he'd ever laid a hand on me. He was drunk."

"That doesn't make it okay, Molly."

"I know." She lowered her head, and I pulled her in for a tight hug.

It felt like I had been on fire for as long as I could remember, and she was a fire extinguisher. Her skin was warm, despite the light chill. Having her that close again lifted a massive weight from my heart.

She shivered against me, but I knew it wasn't from the cold breeze rolling off the water. Something clicked inside of me, and I took her face in my hand and kissed her.

I refused to waste any more of our lives.

Her lips mashed into mine messily. We were groping teenagers again, embracing each other like every breath was our last. It all felt so natural, *so right*. She was the woman of my dreams, and I was her long-lost love.

Not even Disney could write our love story.

Then she tore herself away, and it all came crashing down.

"Take me home," Molly said sullenly, stepping backward with the deliberate lack of cheer that a funeral procession might have.

"Go? I thought we—" I started.

"You were wrong. This was a mistake."

"You're still wearing the bracelet though." I stepped forward, and she kept pace, staying out of my reach. "I don't understand."

Molly sighed, running both hands through her hair.

"I don't wear it as a reminder of how much I loved you. I feel that every day. I know how much I still love you. I wear it as a reminder of the pain I never want to feel again. It doesn't matter that I'm now single. I can't trust you, Luke. You're just going to break my heart like you did before."

"Molly—" I protested.

"I promised myself I'd never let anyone hurt me again." Molly pinched the heart charm between her fingers tightly enough to turn her fingers white. "Especially not you."

CHAPTER 12

Richard

"Morning, criminal." Gloria smiled. She was sitting on one of two benches just outside the police station when I walked out. She had two blessed cups of black heaven, one in either hand.

She was the last person I expected to see this morning.

Gloria wore upper-thigh-length, fashionably ripped shorts, a gray tank top, and a sleeveless denim overshirt without buttons. She tapped the ground with her dark flats, stood up, and handed me a coffee.

"You're a life saver," I said.

"Least I can do. I saw them tow your car and figured you might need a ride out of here."

"I can call for a driver," I said between warm sips of coffee. With a little caffeine in me, I almost felt human again. "I don't want to keep you from the Rocket."

"No such luck, I'm afraid." Gloria shrugged and started for her car in the larger-than-necessary parking lot. "You happened to get arrested before my one day off a week." She lowered her oversized sunglasses and flashed me a look that said she liked what she saw, but also understood I wasn't at my finest either. "Shower or food first?"

"Shower. Definitely shower." I wasn't expecting a Ritz-Carlton, but the holding cell's mattress stank of almost every fluid a human could secrete. I chose to sit in the metal chair for the night instead. That stank much less.

I needed to burn these clothes.

Gloria drove me back to the guesthouse I inhabited at the base of my father's estate.

"Fancy." She whistled, walking into the three-level stucco and stone guesthouse behind me.

"It's all right." I peeled off my ruined overshirt and undershirt, casually tossing them on the floor near the trash can.

"Are you hungry?" Gloria asked, dragging a hand over the polished marble countertop. Her eyes licked up my naked torso. My broad chest and abs were still bulging from the sets of push-ups and sit-ups I did in the holding cell.

When there was no chance of sleep, it was the only way to keep myself occupied.

"I could eat." My eyes returned the favor, dragged

down her petite form and milky exposed legs. I *was* hungry. The last thing I'd eaten was her. It didn't fill me up, but it sure as hell was satisfying.

Deciding against letting my cock fully wake until I'd at least taken a shower, I thought of all the colors and smells coming out of the cell's backed-up toilet.

That killed my hard-on immediately.

I'd have to remember that particular horror show if I was going to be spending any more time with Gloria in public.

I was arrested at the worst possible time. We were so close to actually having sex that it frustrated the hell out of my body. One way or another, I needed to vent this pent-up sexual frustration.

I used my time in the shower to both clean up and get myself off. I was finding it harder and harder to think straight with Gloria around. The water streamed over me as I stroked my thick cock. In the privacy of the shower, I was free to remember everything I'd forced out of my head in jail.

I had to slam a palm up against the wall to keep my strength through the fantasy. Gloria's smooth thighs were split over my shoulders and the warm, wonderful taste of her pussy in my mouth. I imagined what it'd be like to slip my swollen head inside those tight lower lips of hers and fuck her till she couldn't walk.

I came soon after.

Drying myself off, I struggled coming to a decision about Gloria. I dressed in thin khakis and a linen shirt—something light and breezy for summer—and began to plan.

I liked to plan things out. I liked control in all things. When I had a clear path to what I wanted, everything in my life made sense.

I wanted to win the inheritance. More than that, I wanted to *crush* my brother. I would figure out a way to get him back for what he did to me, but *to really win* I'd have to get a girl pregnant.

That was the real problem.

I wanted to be a father... eventually. But it would have to be with the right woman, a woman I truly cared about. For as much as I wanted to win, the thought of bringing a child into the world out of obligation instead of love made me feel hollow and sick inside.

Then again, the clock was ticking. If something happened to Dad, we'd both lose everything. It was too dark a thought to dwell on for long.

Dammit, Dad.

Why did you do this?

I bedded whoever I wanted without risk or attachment, easily moving from woman to woman. I did it all on my own terms, in full control.

I liked my life!

Feeling sorry for myself wasn't going to change anything.

The first step was to find a woman who wanted kids, especially in the immediate future. Unfortunately, that eliminated Gloria right off the bat. My heart sank a little.

Gloria was just a pleasant distraction, one I'd have to get rid of if I wanted to seriously beat Lucas.

I walked into the kitchen fully dressed, swabbing the last bit of water out of my ears with a small towel I kept on my shoulder. I could smell that Gloria was cooking something, maybe even *several* somethings. When I finally turned the corner, I saw that the countertop, stove, and sink were full of pots, pans, dishes, and utensils.

Had she used every piece of cookware I had?

"Hey," she said, looking a bit flustered. "I started making some eggs, but I think your stupid oven is busted."

"It's just unplugged." I laughed. "All of this was for eggs?"

"That's what it started as. Then I looked up a quick recipe to make in the microwave, but that came out like garbage." Gloria had the water running and was washing some of the messy dishes. "I just said the hell with it and ordered some food through the Foodler app on my phone."

I laughed again, walking over to give her a hand cleaning up. "You didn't have to make anything."

"I'm usually a good cook!" she protested "I just…. I don't know what happened. I blame your kitchen. I think it hates me."

"You're probably right. It hates me too." I rolled up my sleeves, stood next to her, and took a large glass casserole dish into the empty sink. Her shoulder brushed against my elbow and sent goose bumps up my arm. I swallowed away the notion that forgetting about Gloria would be easy. "So what's for breakfast?"

"I hope you like Chinese food." Her smirk had a tinge of self-consciousness about it. It was actually kind of cute. "I couldn't find any diners that delivered."

"I'm just impressed you found a Chinese place open at nine thirty in the morning."

Almost like clockwork, when we finished doing the dishes, the food arrived.

"So what did they end up charging you with?" Gloria asked with half a mouthful of fried rice sometime later.

She'd ordered a small mountain of food, which was good because I didn't realize how hungry I was until I could smell it. I didn't answer her until I downed half a container's worth of beef pad thai. "Possession with intent to sell."

Gloria smiled mischievously. There was a glinting spark in her gray eyes. "Who'd of thought you had a wild streak in you?"

I opened my mouth to explain that it was my brother's doing, and because it was only a little over the limit and it being my first offense—and who my family was—I was most likely going to get the charges dropped. Maybe I'd have to pay a fine.

I was going to tell her all that, but I kept quiet and shrugged instead.

Let her think what she wants, I thought with a thrill.

I was always a bad boy in my own right, but I'd never

been the wild one. That was always Lucas. Breaking the law and living by your own rules was liberating; I could see why it was so compelling to Lucas.

We chatted lightly as we finished our meal. When I put my chopsticks down triumphantly, the mountain of food was just scattered wreckage.

"Who was that guy at your party? The one that looked like the dirty biker version of Fabio?"

"Lucas," I replied, wiping my mouth with a napkin. "My brother."

"Ah." Gloria pushed a small battered piece of chicken across her plate idly. "I take it you two don't get along."

"That's a bit of an understatement."

"What's the deal with you two? I have an older sister out in Washington, and yeah, we fight a lot on holidays, but who cares? We're family. Why do you hate each other so much?"

The topic had come up a few times, and each time I was able to redirect it. It was hard for me to open up to strangers, even the ones I liked. The absurdity of my father's game was one thing. That was recent and still didn't fully feel real. My baggage with Lucas was an entirely different thing that quietly simmered between us for decades. Talking about that was much more difficult.

"We have our reasons," I said cryptically. Gloria scowled at me. I sighed, lounged back into the couch, and accepted that she wasn't going to let it go this time.

"Lucas is everything I'm not." I paused and attempted to clarify. "Lucas… he should've been so much more. He's naturally talented in many ways, not just with music."

"Wait, Lucas King… Lucky Luke from Gunmetal Tears?" I could see the realization dawn on her, followed by a feeling of foolishness that she didn't figure it out sooner. "How do you mean *should've been more*? Those guys had a few bestselling albums! Well… back when they were still together. Not many people can pull off the whole rock-star thing."

This wasn't coming out right.

Gloria quickly texted a message then set her phone back down.

I could talk for hours about so many things, but my family was not one of them. It was easier for me to compartmentalize all that pain and anger, push it away, and focus on other things that were important, like running my business.

"I worked my ass off for my degree in some of the toughest schools in the world, then had huge shoes to fill when my father got sick and couldn't run the family company anymore.

"My brother should have been right there with me the whole way. My father prepared us to take over an empire together, and when the time came, Lucas wouldn't answer the call. He'd rather go off, do drugs, and be a waste than to uphold the King legacy."

"Who's to say the King legacy ends at business?"

Gloria asked, playing the devil's advocate.

"That's how we are though. For generations, the King family ran businesses. Ever since the eighteen hundreds when Gerald King came to America with the fleet of ships he owned."

"Gunmetal Tears were a big deal for their genre. Your brother definitely built something there."

"That's just a flash in the pan." I waved it off, not able or willing to hide my disdain for his band. "Everything I struggled with in high school, he just breezed through. Lucas could've been every bit the businessman I am, probably even more so. He's naturally cunning and brilliant, but would rather squander that immense potential than use it for anything productive."

"I don't know.... It sounds like he's just doing what he loves."

There's doing what you love, then there's being selfish.

After everything our father did for him, taking a stake in the family business was the least he could do. If anyone should understand what it was like to be a part of something greater, it should've been Lucas. He'd be nothing right now if it wasn't for my father.

And he repays him by abandoning everything the King family stands for?

For as mad at Lucas as I was, I couldn't tell Gloria any of *that*.

"Your sister in Washington—" Instead, it was better to just change the subject. "—what does she do?"

"She's married to a navy seaman and has two kids." Gloria snorted in exasperation. She must not approve of the guy her sister was with. "*That's* what she does."

Gloria's phone vibrated. It was a text from a friend.

"Looks like Lucky Luke is playing an acoustic show this Friday at the...." Gloria's face screwed up like she'd drank some spoiled milk.

"What is it?"

"He's playing at the *Family Room*. I thought they shut that cesspit down." She glanced up at me then added, "It's this shitty run-down venue the next town over that's been around way too long and needs to get bulldozed."

"I take it you're not a fan?"

"Absolutely not. The owners are assholes. It's got a reputation for letting minors drink. My friend's underage sister left there drunk one night and wrapped her car around a tree."

I wanted to ask if the girl was all right, but the dark expression on Gloria's face told me she wasn't.

"Sorry to hear that," I said. During the lull in conversation that followed, a wicked idea came to me. "Are you free Friday?"

"Hmm." Gloria thought about it, then shrugged. "I should be able to have Judy cover for me. What do you have in mind?"

"Payback."

CHAPTER 13

"What's up, guys? I'm from Gunmetal Tears. They call me Lucky Luke," I said into the microphone at the Family Room.

The packed house lost their fucking minds.

I felt the vibration of their screaming worship deep in my chest. It made me smile. This was my first time back on stage in years. There was this ferocious energy you got while you perform; it was a drug all its own.

I knew a lot of guys who chased that high off stage and never lived to tell about it.

Music was always different for me. It wasn't about a god complex. It wasn't about the money or prestige, or even fucking whoever you wanted. It was about releasing all the anger, pain, hope, and love that threatened to tear me apart now that Molly was gone.

It was the same reason I started playing professionally to begin with.

I ran my fingers through the frets of my Fender guitar and began to strum out the opening to our first number one hit. The guitar and mic were hooked into the same acoustic amplifier stack; otherwise they'd have been lost to the roar of the nearly two hundred people packed into this club.

Sadness, discord, longing, and rage—our dark melancholy rock tapped into the pain that so many other people felt when they lost someone they loved. Was it really such a wonder that our songs resonated with so many people?

To fuck up and hurt people was all so *human.*

The first song bled into the second, then the third, then the fourth. My fingers ached from a lack of practice. It had been a long time since I played any of these songs even privately. I didn't need to play them often anymore to do them justice. The notes, the words, it was all just as much a part of me as the nose on my face.

One of the two color-changing spotlights on me popped loudly, then went dark. I'd never played the Family Room before. The place was a fucking joke. I was told that it used to be an Italian restaurant twenty years ago. In that time, all they'd done to the place was tear out the seating to open it up into a big hall.

The only modern thing about it was the sprinkler system that was no doubt forced onto the owner.

That was one of the few things I always checked in person when I booked a gig. No pyrotechnics and a working sprinkler installed. As long as the venue was safe for my fans, I couldn't give a shit about the color of the M&Ms backstage.

Honestly, I didn't give a damn about the room's natural acoustics or even about the audio quality. My style always had a dirty sound to begin with. I was glad they liked the music, but I didn't play for my fans.

I played for myself. This was my church. Molly was my god, and this was how I prayed to her.

I hadn't talked to her since I dropped her off after the party. I spent that night outside, about a block away, keeping vigil over her in case her asshole soon-to-be ex-husband came back.

He didn't.

The following week, I kept my distance and watched over her silently in a rented car. The inheritance war was on in full. Dick and I fucked with each other as much as possible. I spread rumors that he had gonorrhea; he made sure that every time I stepped into a public place I was mobbed with people which made it impossible to do fucking anything.

We were little boys throwing toys at each other and sneaking painful jabs in when the adults were out of the room, except we were all grown up and could do far worse than throw tantrums.

The thought of fucking anyone but Molly now that she was single felt like a betrayal, even if she didn't want me anymore. For as ruthless and corporate as Dick was, I was still pretty sure he wasn't going to knock some random girl up to win a bet.

We were at a stalemate, so we just made the other's life as miserable as possible.

"Fuck all this shit." Halfway through my fifth song I stopped. I couldn't do it. I couldn't mindlessly play Gunmetal's hits. All I did this past week was watch over Molly and write music. I barely ate or slept.

"You guys want to hear something new, something bloody, something downright heartbreaking?" I walked the stage, pausing between certain words to thrust the mic toward the audience.

The crowd cheered after *new, bloody,* and *heartbreaking.* Cell phone cameras switched from flash to record. There were a few songs and stories kicking around in my mind and heart, but nothing was finished enough to be recorded yet.

In the grand scheme of things, it didn't matter. I had no idea what I was going to say or play. I opened my mouth and let out the words that I needed to get rid of.

"I wanna tell you a quick story of this prick I knew once. Let's call him...." I set the mic on the one stool in the middle of the stage and took a long drag of the beer that was resting there. "*Unlucky* Luke."

The crowd laughed.

"Luke once knew this girl. Dark haired, dark eyed, bright souled. You always hear about the one that got away." I plucked at my strings somberly. "But I'm not talking about her. I'm talking about the one he stupidly *pushed* away.

Seasons turned to dust and memories, stars fell from the sky, and the fiery heart that led his way cooled and quieted." I walked my fingers higher up on the guitar's neck like a hangman's noose as I played. "Y'see he waited too long.

Waiting is a game for fools, and Unlucky Luke was their *king*!"

I couldn't tell when it happened, but at some point my speaking voice had become my singing voice. I hadn't planned on playing Molly's song. It was like a cough that itched the bottom of my lungs; it needed to come out.

"Fate stole him, but fear *kept* him. He won every battle, but lost every war. Time and victory defeated him."

I strummed hard, squeezing the head stock tightly just below the tuners and let the instrument hang by one hand. The thrum choked off into a flat, uncomfortable sound. I didn't wear a strap so the motion gave the effect that the gallows had given way and the guitar hung by its neck until dead.

"When he finally came home to his castle, someone else had already fallen out of his throne. All she wanted was love."

I snapped up the guitar and started playing again. The sound was rough and loud, discordant at first; then it settled into a fast melodic rhythm.

"The king of fools should've moved heaven itself—" My hands moved automatically, continuing the same melody, but my words broke off when I saw Dick enter with the dark-haired girl I saw him with at the party.

Were they a thing? Thoughts of losing to Dick twisted my stomach into a knot.

Right behind the smug-looking couple, another man walked in. He had a dark, formal uniform and badge, but no gun. The man didn't look happy. When he pulled a pad out of his breast pocket, I realized he wasn't a cop.

He was a *fire marshal*.

The only thing fully up to code on this place was the sprinkler system, and that was probably done only to avoid suspicion. How the Family Room snuck under the radar with everything else for so long was a testament to the power of bribes.

This place was about to go down. *Hard.*

There was a burst of movement behind me. I snapped a glance over and saw the club's owner run out the back entrance where the bands loaded in their gear. He realized he was fucked and decided to escape and cut his losses. By the speed he was running, there must've been more going down than selling beer to minors.

He must've been selling drugs too.

On the way out, that unbelievable prick pulled the fire alarm.

Well, that is one way to ensure people don't chase

after you.

That new sprinkler system sputtered for half a second then rocketed into action; water seemed to rain down in buckets. I immediately stopped playing as a look of abject terror washed over the crowd.

For the second time in one night, the crowd lost their minds, but this time for a darker reason. There wasn't any fire, but there was a real threat that people could be hurt by trampling.

"Everyone, calm down!" I shouted through my microphone. The water hadn't knocked out the power to my speakers yet. Even with the added amplification, my words were still only barely audible over the frenzy of fear. "There is no fire!"

Both Richard and the fire marshal were doing their best to herd the horde of people through the open double doors. The utter mistake of Richard's timing was written all over his face.

He thought he'd close the place down as I was on stage and make me look like an asshole for not completing the show. It actually wasn't a bad plan. Unfortunately, he had no idea it would turn into a goddamn riot.

I wanted to jump down and help the people who fell, but I'd just be adding another body to the chaos. I stayed on the stage and tried to calm everyone as best I could. I told them a fire marshal was already here. I told them where the exits were and to pick up the damn people they pushed over.

For nearly five minutes, it was madness in that little club. It took so much longer for people to get out of there than it should've. I shivered to think what the place would've been like had it really been on fire.

The thought made me nauseous.

Soon enough the last of the stragglers walked or were helped out the door. Fortunately, it didn't look like anyone was hurt too badly. No one had to be carried out, *thank Christ!*

The sprinklers never stopped. I was soaked to the bone as I did a final sweep to make sure no one was trapped anywhere or needed help.

And for a short time, I was the only person left inside the sad, waterlogged building.

I stepped back up on the stage and attempted to finish my song to Molly.

The mechanical rainfall had long since shorted out my amp and ruined all my equipment. The guitar wasn't electric, so I ripped out the chord and continued to play. The hollow laminated spruce and mahogany body filled with water, making the guitar heavy and giving the music a tinny sound. The coarse strings made my water-wrinkled fingers bleed.

I still couldn't find it in myself to stop.

"The king of fools should've moved heaven itself *to get her back,*" I sang to no one.

In a movie, Molly would've walked in, heard my song and seen me soaked and pitiful. We'd have met halfway in a sweeping hug, then I would've kissed her under the fake rain.

Half a dozen separate sirens rapidly closed in from every direction.

Looking out over the deserted hall, I truly felt empty inside. Had there actually been a fire, I didn't know that I'd even have tried to leave.

I played until blood ran down my arms and one of my strings snapped. Then I played some more. My tears mingled invisibly with the falling water.

Finally a thick, gloved hand of a fireman landed gently on my shoulder. "C'mon, son. It's all over. It's time to go."

CHAPTER 14

Richard

"Leave the bottle," I said, checking my watch.

The waiter nodded. He finished topping my glass off, then set the expensive bottle of something French down on the table.

My date for the evening, Madison Grace, was the governor's daughter. I sipped my glass more quickly than was probably wise. The night—and this date— was far from over. I felt a sense of exhaustion at the thought of finishing it.

Madison had been in the bathroom for what felt like an hour.

The appetizers came, got cold, and were taken away. Any moment the entrees would be here. I asked the waiter if they had anything Asian inspired, but he respectfully gave me his regrets and said there wasn't.

What I wouldn't give for some average Chinese

food on my couch with Gloria right now. I sighed, feeling a pang of regret.

The wine helped with that. I drained the rest of the glass.

The time for distractions was over.

The Family Room fiasco showed me a lot of things. Above all, it showed me what kind of fool I was.

I was so wrapped up in petty revenge, I let my pride get the best of me. I could've brought the fire marshal there well before the show, but I wanted to humiliate Lucas instead.

Because of that, people got hurt.

Gloria got hurt….

She was standing near the doors when the crowd burst through. She'd already been kicked and stepped on several times before I was able to pull her out of the flood of people. She shouldn't have been there.

I never should've let any of that happen.

The harsh spike of her scream rattled through my head more often than not. All I could think about was what would've happened had I not reached her in time.

It scared the hell out of me.

I set my empty glass roughly down on the table and snapped off its stem. My hand was shaking when I let the now-useless wine glass fall to the floor.

The tables were fairly private—as they should've been considering the cost of this place—but that didn't stop some heads from craning over to see the source of the sound and my cursing.

Within seconds, someone came over with a replacement, apologizing profusely for the defective glass. There was nothing wrong with the wine glass. Both of my knuckles had turned white from my balled-up fists.

I was lucky it didn't shatter in my hands.

I rubbed a hand over my face, reminding myself that Gloria was fine. I had rushed her to the nearest hospital. She only had two sprained ribs and a concussion thankfully.

Sitting in the waiting room, I realized I was going about everything backwards. I shouldn't be trying to *hurt* my brother; I should be trying to *beat* him.

There was only one way to do that.

I left Gloria a letter the following day, ending whatever it was that we had—if what we had was anything at all. Maybe in a different time *or life*, things could've worked out between us. There was no changing the facts.

She didn't want kids right now, and right now was when I needed one.

It was a bitterly hard pill to swallow, but it was necessary. I was going to win this challenge, not because I needed the inheritance, but because Lucas didn't deserve it. He lost that privilege when he burned the opportunity I gave him.

The King legacy was too important and needed to be preserved.

Lucas was too selfish to understand that.

That's why I refused to play this game with him any longer. There needed to be a winner and a loser as quickly as possible, because next time we fought, someone like Gloria could get hurt.

I couldn't live with myself if I let that happen.

I spent every evening since with a new woman. So far none had been an appropriate fit. The dates always ended shortly after dinner. Gloria was still too fresh in my mind to take any of them home with me.

I looked into the glass of dark red wine. It was the same color as Gloria's lipstick.

I smiled thinking back to the night she gave me the private tour of both her coffee shop and her milky, smooth body.

And she said she was a terrible tour guide....

I had seen Gloria half a dozen more times after she'd picked me up from the police station. Each date was exhilarating and wonderfully different. We shouldn't have been able to mesh together as well as we did. She was quirky, rude, impulsive, and opinionated—my opposite in many ways.

Gloria was beautiful in a way I'd never seen before. In eastern philosophies, she'd have been the yin to my yang. Here, however, she was only an unforgettable memory that I would carry with me for the rest of my life.

In my darker moments, I would hate that she couldn't be both.

"I am so sorry, darling." Madison materialized.

Her immaculate, long, golden hair was done into an exquisite updo. She wore a floor-length maroon ball gown and enough diamond jewelry to fund a small nation. I stood up and got her chair for her. "Time simply slipped away from me. Where were we?"

"You were telling me about your father, I believe."

"Oh yes! We were discussing his reelection fundraiser campaign." Madison's face lit up.

Joy.

The waiter arrived just in time with our entrees to divert the conversation once more. I couldn't wait for the dinner to be over. Madison hadn't been particularly awful or anything, just *ordinary.*

Madison, like every other girl I'd seen this week, had been more of the same. They all came from money; they ran various video or traditional blogs about fashion or modeling and tended to discuss the important or successful work their parents did.

Had Gloria ruined these women for me by virtue of being different and exciting?

Madison had been the most tolerable thus far though. She'd at least been through college, a psychology major at that. And although she didn't outright say it, it appeared she wanted to follow in her father's footsteps and go into a career in politics.

Politics was generally a little too slimy for me, but it was a nice divergence to the hollow, empty conversations I'd had with other women this week.

I didn't think it was going to work out with Madison

either, but we'd probably take the scenic route, instead of the highway, when I dropped her off after dinner.

"I would, if you don't mind of course, like to dispense with the pleasantries and discuss the parameters necessary for my impregnation." Madison cut a small piece of her duck.

"Beg your pardon?" I coughed, nearly spitting out my bite of filet mignon.

She casually chewed and swallowed, then touched the cloth napkin to the corner of her mouth and cleaned a mess that wasn't there.

"My menstrual cycle is exactly twenty-eight days, with my day of ovulation arriving in the middle of each month."

"I don't mean to sound rude, Madison." I forced down my bite of steak and chased it with a long gulp of wine. "Why are we talking about this?"

"Your father's will, silly." She smiled like a talk show host, cocking her head slightly. Not one strand of her perfect hair so much as flitted out of place. "I assume because we're meeting at all, my genetic makeup is acceptable."

"Hold on." I leaned forward in a harsh whisper. I only told Gloria about this, and I doubted she was the gossiping type. "How do you know about my father's will?"

"I keep my ears open for whispers. News travels fast." Madison seemed to alternate between data analyst and valley girl with astonishing ease. She shrugged.

"Some news travels faster than others."

"I don't know what you might've heard—" I started, feeling a little on the defensive. The arrangement between my father, Lucas, and I wasn't something I wanted getting around.

"Oh posh." Madison waved a hand dismissively. She winked at me and gave me a knowing smile. "I'm the daughter of a politician. Your secret's safe with me."

Madison was perfect, uncomfortably so.

She had this *curated* feel to her, like everything she wore, did, said, and even the way she moved was all decided on by a committee. Madison was perfect *by design*. She was a child's plastic doll that had just been removed from its packaging.

Was this what it was like to be a politician?

She was the exact opposite of Gloria's rough-around-the-edges, brutally honest, take-no-prisoners attitude.

"May we get started?" she asked.

"By all means," I said, curious as to what *get started* meant. I leaned back in my chair and watched in awe as she pulled out a thick folder from her purse. The folder and the paper inside of it was half the traditional size, so that it could fit in her purse.

That definitely wasn't in there before, I thought. Did she have that packet stashed somewhere here?

Was that why she was gone for so long?

"Here we are," she said with the tone and focus of

a woman who enjoyed doing her own taxes. She slid the document across the table for me to review. I riffled through it as she talked. "I have it all laid out here. Blue-tabbed pages in the front are social events so we can gradually introduce ourselves to the public as a couple. The wedding preparation and ceremony are pages seventeen through thirty—"

"What's this in the back? The red section." I'd read novels shorter than this manuscript. It was also written mostly in legalese, which was both off-putting and impressive. My attorneys would be reviewing this to make sure I kept both my kidneys.

"That is how we met." She smiled again as if remembering the day fondly. "It was a warm summer evening in Vienna. You were on a break between college semesters, and I'd flown in to visit my father. We met through a mutual friend at an intimate cocktail party."

"We met at the country club party a few weeks ago," I said flatly, my eyes narrowing at her blatant lie.

"That timeline," Madison said the word as if the truth was just one of many reasonable options to choose from, "wouldn't be socially acceptable if you plan on beating your brother to that which is rightly yours."

"Rightly mine?" My lips pressed together, forming a thin line across my face. How much did she know about my family?

"Well, of course." Her face brightened. "You've followed in your father's footsteps and expanded his already impressive empire. Lucas on the other hand—" Her eyebrows rose, and her lips fell disapprovingly. "—Lucas played guitar in a band that is no longer relevant."

Madison's change in expression was so subtle that unless you were looking for it, you'd miss it. So she did have emotions under there somewhere.

I was just glad she didn't know about my mother's affair or about Lucas actually being my *half* brother. I didn't like my brother, but there was something in the way she talked about him that bothered me.

It was a weird, juvenile emotion. It was all right if I beat Lucas up and humiliated him, but I didn't like it when others did it in my presence.

"What's in this for you, Madison? It's obviously not the money you're after."

"*Status*, darling," she said softly, her lips snapping back into their inoffensive smile. "I plan on running for Senate eventually. I've done my research on you, Richard. Unlike your vagabond brother, you kept your public image clean and professional and your promiscuous nature very discrete. I can appreciate that."

Madison waived the waiter over, ordered a glass of dark juice, then continued. "You're widely regarded as a leader and a man to be respected. You'll make for a perfect political spouse."

"You're making quite the assumption, Madison." I took a sip of wine. She had a lot of sound points, but everything was so mechanical.

It was odd that I suddenly disliked stark pragmatism.

That's because it's boring, said a small voice in my head that sounded a lot like Gloria.

"Why exactly should I pick you?" I asked, reeling my drifting mind back in and focusing on Madison. I had an entire town to choose from.

Why should I pick her?

"I'm your only real choice." Madison looked genuinely confused. I didn't see what was so obvious to her. She leaned in closer to spell it out for me.

Madison began rattling off the women I'd seen so far this week. "Paige and Veronica are secretly addicted to various drugs. Kelsey is infertile due to a car accident. Brittany plays on the other team, but was put up to your date by her father. That leaves only Hailey. She's your best bet, but her family's poor reputation is sure to affect the King brand negatively."

I said nothing. I knew some of that was true just from the interactions I had with them.

"Were you spying on me?"

"Lord no!" Madison's chuckle bordered on genuine. "Who has the time for that sort of thing? I just have a lot of vigilant friends. Those same friends learned something about your brother as well. Would you like to know?"

I rolled my hand forward, indicating her to continue. I hated spectacle and subterfuge, they reminded me too much of work.

"Lucas has been busy as well." Madison dangled the information like a fisherman casting a line. "The night of your party, while you were out gallivanting with the coffeehouse barista, Lucas disappeared out in the woods with the love of his life. It's only a matter of time until he gets her pregnant accidentally or otherwise.

"Pardon my boldness, Richard. Frankly speaking, you're running out of time." Madison tried and mostly succeeded at suppressing her proud smile. "You do want to win, don't you?"

She could see in my eyes that I wanted to win. There wasn't sadistic satisfaction in her features; she was just a woman who could recognize and capture opportunity when it came along.

Madison was a shark that swam with dolphins.

"I'll need the evening to review your proposal." This felt like a hostile takeover. I didn't like being manipulated.

"Of course." She spoke with the practiced indifference of a news anchor fluidly changing topics from a deadly house fire to a puff piece on this year's poodle hairstyles. "Dessert?"

In the back of my head, my analytical side forced me to look at the facts. Madison really was the best option. I was letting my pride get in the way of progress.

You're not doing this for love, I scolded myself.

I left Gloria to win.

If I hesitated now, then I left her for nothing.

"My father's hosting a dinner next weekend; I'd like you to join me." I paid for our meal and held her chair for her.

"Lovely," she said, bowing her head slightly. It was a submissive gesture to bolster my confidence in having made the right decision.

"Shall I take you home?"

"No need. I have a car waiting here. Sex isn't necessary for thirteen days. I've already sent you a calendar update through your phone."

I raised an eyebrow, then checked my email. There it was—her fertility cycle, *all of it*. She'd also gone so far as planning out the optimal times and *positions* for intercourse.

Madison was a psychology major; I'd have to remember that.

CHAPTER 15

Lucas

There was a knock at my door.

"Leave it!" I shouted at housekeeping from the bathroom as I turned off the shower. Twice a day they dropped off food for me at my father's request.

It'd been a long time since I needed someone to take care of me, but I could tell it made him happy to do it, so I didn't complain.

I was going to find a place outside of town; Dad wouldn't hear it. He booked me an indefinite suite at the hotel he owned a few minutes' drive from the main drag. It was the tallest building around, and I was staying on the top floor.

I had a great view of most of the valley but spent most of my time watching the Matt Baker Elementary school for signs of Molly or motorcycles. She often stayed late, and I was always ready to rush over there at the first sign of trouble. Part of me was disappointed that trouble never came.

Selfish, I know, but it'd at least be a chance to see her again.

The knocking sounded again.

They were insistent today.

I brushed my hair back and wrapped the towel around my waist. I was still dripping wet when I decided to answer it. Maybe there was a problem with billing or a maintenance call or something.

I swung the door open and was about to point out the Do Not Disturb sign hanging on the door, but all the steam went out of my aggravation when I saw who it was.

"Hi," Molly said, adjusting her glasses. She wore a red button-down blouse, slacks, and sneakers. Her brown hair was pinned up but had the telltale flyaways of a long day out of the house. She must have come right over after work.

"Molly," I exclaimed, jerking backward so suddenly that my towel unfastened around my waist. "Shit." I caught it, then shouldered open the closing door to keep it from slamming in her face. "Hi. Come in."

After everything that happened, she was the last person I expected to see.

"Did I catch you at a bad time?" She let her gaze drop briefly to the corded muscles of my lower stomach. The V in my hips showed more and more as I bunched the towel ineffectually.

Define bad?

Richard just announced he was seeing some politician's daughter formally. I saw a picture of the girl; she looked fake and plastic like an inflatable doll given life. I wondered what happened with the girl with the short, spiky, black hair he was hanging out with. I was surprised they were together as long as they were; she didn't strike me as his type.

Fuck it, I guess it didn't matter. If he was formally with this new blonde chick, that wasn't good for me.

"Nah, I'm good. Everything's good," I lied, holding the door open for her. "Are you all right?"

"I'm all right," she said, looking around. There was something off about her voice. Was she lying too?

"Hold on a sec." I found a clean pair of jeans in the back hallway and threw them on just out of sight. "How did you find me? I'm not listed downstairs."

"*Elmo* is." Molly peeked into the hallway, hoping to catch a peek but was too late. There was a spark of cunning in her eyes.

I snorted, zipping up my fly with a smile. *Clever as always.* I spotted a shirt but left it. Let her see me half naked. She used to like it when I went shirtless, and from the lusty look in her eyes, I could tell she still did.

It didn't hurt that I put on twenty pounds of solid muscle since the last time she saw me.

"Jesus, your hands!" Molly glared worriedly at my bandaged fingers. "Is that from the fire?"

"There was no fire. It looks worse than it is." I wiggled

my fingers, then let my smile fade. "Why are you here, Molly?"

"I can leave if you want." She frowned and made her way to the couch, looking worried about something. How worried did she have to be to seek me out?

The vivid image of her getting slapped outside the Black Chains MC was burned into my head. Was she in some kind of trouble?

I grabbed her a bottle of water from the fridge then joined her.

"Last time we were together, you made it pretty clear you didn't want to see me ever again. Are you sure everything's all right?" I studied her, looking for bruises. "If that piece of shit touched you again, I swear to God—"

"It's not that." Molly reached out and put a hand on my knee. The warmth in her touch struck me like a blow. Fuck, I missed her. I missed this. I missed everything about my old life with her. "I heard your song, well, most of it."

"My song?" I hadn't published anything new in years. What was she talking about?

"Your performance at the Family Room." She tucked a lock of hair behind her ear, half of which got stuck behind the earpiece of her glasses. "It's all over YouTube."

"You mean *your* song," I corrected.

"Yeah, I guess so. It was beautiful. I'd like to hear the end of it." She smiled, showcasing a glimmer of hope on a face that was prettier than any song I could ever write. "The video cut out when the sprinklers went on."

"It's not finished," I said. "I don't have an ending for it yet."

I'd been locked away for days obsessively writing and rewriting the ending. I wanted it to be perfect, but just couldn't get it there. If it was perfect, maybe, *just maybe*, she might come back to me.

"Oh." There was a hint of disappointment in her voice that made my heart crack. It took everything I had not to reach out and touch her, to soothe that look away. "I don't want to hate you, Luke. I'm hurt and pissed off, but that doesn't undo all the good memories I have of you. I just want to understand."

"Know that despite everything that's happened"—I put my arm over the back of the sofa and lean in—"I never stopped caring about you."

"Why did you leave me?" Her voice was so quiet.

"I—" I pushed my air out in resignation, thinking of the promise I made to my mother. "I can't tell you. I'm sorry."

My fingers twitched at how close she was. I *needed* to touch her, to prove to myself that she was really here. When my hand grazed the side of her face I realized how lost I was. "I'm back now, though. And I'm never leaving you again. I promise."

In the diffused light of late afternoon, Molly's subtle freckles glowed like stars. I didn't care if it took me the rest of my life, I'd memorize every single one of them.

"How can I trust you?" Molly's eyelids got heavier as I closed in.

"You can't." My hand slipped behind her neck, and I pulled her soft lips against mine, kissing her so passionately that it stole our breath for a moment afterward. "But I'm going to change that. I promise."

The tension, the yearning, the longing, all of it popped like an overfilled balloon. I slid my other hand around her back in a tight hug and picked her up off the couch. Our mouths parting barely enough to take in air, I carried her into the dining room.

Neither of us could resist the gravity of each other, and we crashed together with a sense of inevitability. It was like fate was screaming at us, "This was how it always should've been!"

Why did it take us so fucking long to see that?

CHAPTER 16

Lucas

"We shouldn't be doing this," Molly said, between kisses and gasps as I sat her down on the hardwood dinner table I never ate at.

"You're right." In a big sweeping motion, I cleared the large table of the clothes, mail, and music sheets it had accumulated.

We were raw, damaged, and emotionally vulnerable. Sex would probably only complicate things between us. We should take things slower, catch up with each other and feel things out.

Knowing something and being able to do it were two radically different things.

Molly popped open the buttons down the front of her blouse as quickly as possible. I unclasped her bra, then put my hands over her hot, olive shoulders and guided all the fabric off her.

I still couldn't believe how fucking good she looked now.

I carried around a few pictures of us when we were younger, but they paled in comparison to the woman she became. I stayed off social media once I found out that she had been married. What was the point?

I'd have agonized over every happy photo of her and her husband, wishing—*knowing*—it should've been me instead.

I laid her back on the dark wood finish; it complemented her radiant skin and highlighted her every sexy curve. The soft curls of her brown hair spread across the table like a sunburst, outlining her further. She stretched her arms out, reaching for me, dragging me down into her.

My cock throbbed at the sight of her.

It was like tumbling into a dream while you were still awake. Nothing else mattered in the world but her. For the rest of the night, she was all mine again.

It had been well over a year since the last time I'd been laid. It always felt wrong for some reason and never satisfied me. Since coming back and seeing her, I had to jerk off half a dozen times a day.

I should've asked if she was ready for this, but the look in her eyes told me everything I needed to know. She bit her lip and jutted her chin forward, beckoning me. Molly didn't hide how badly she wanted this.

She sucked in air when I lay against her. Her perky

nipples were firm nubs that pressed into my hard pecs. Her hand slid down my ribs, reaching my waistband, and hesitated. A moment of doubt flashed across her face.

"Are you all right?" I asked.

Molly swallowed, then nodded. Her fingers popped the button on my jeans and worked my zipper down carefully.

I wanted to ask if she trusted me, but I kissed her neck instead. I was too worried at what she might say. My own doubts surfaced but were quickly squashed when I smelled her perfume. It was stronger than it should've been this late in the day. She must've put it on before she came over.

It was put on just for me....

Was she hoping this would happen?

I cupped her pussy over her thin work slacks. I could feel her scorching heat flare at my building pressure; it made my cock hard enough to shatter solid marble. I imagined her lower lips glossy with wet anticipation.

Her breathing quickened as she moaned softly, nervous excitement in her eyes. I smoothly unclasped and took down her pants, pulling off her sneakers in the process.

I kissed up her tan legs and dipped my face into her honeypot.

"Fuck," Molly exhaled the word as if it was punched out of her.

She creamed the second she felt my lips on her

inner thigh. I left her white panties on but pulled them aside. All her exquisite beauty was presented before me like a feast to a starving man. It was almost unfair that every part of her looked this amazing.

My whole mouth moved up and through her delicious slit; her muscles trembled against my tongue.

We've never gone this far before, the seventeen-year-old version of me screamed in the back of my head. I had seen and even played with her tits a little before I left, but never anything like this. Not even my wildest fantasies could capture how drunk I'd become off the taste of her pussy.

Her legs twitched as I spelled her name with my tongue against her pussy. A jolt ran through her as she felt my teeth graze against her sensitive clit.

Molly moaned as my swirling tongue explored her every hidden fold. Feeling her quiver against my touch stoked a wildfire inside of me. I had to tightly squeeze my cock to keep it in check.

When she came, all her muscles contracted. Her heels dug into the table so hard that it lifted her ass into a high arc. I followed the wave of her ecstasy, licking and sucking until she cried out for me to stop.

"Oh fuck…." Molly smiled, draping her arm over her blushing face.

"We're not finished," I declared. Peeling her arm off her face, I locked my fingers around her nipple and squeezed. Molly smiled deviously and slid her hand into my pants.

I kissed her. I let her taste what had driven me so wild. She was panting when I pulled away. I could feel her heart racing through her wrist, which I had pinned to the table.

"I guess not…." Her eyes widened as she ran her hand down my thick trunk. My cock was too long for her to reach the head from her angle. "Were you always this big?"

"Scared?"

"No," Molly protested, her lips curled in a half smile. "It's just been a little while."

"I'll go slow." I let my pants fall to my feet and stepped out of them. Then I realized something and cursed to myself.

"What is it?"

I looked up at her, my lips pressed in a tight line. "I don't have any fucking condoms."

Why would I? I sure as hell wasn't expecting any of this, and I wasn't about to hook up with some random bar slut.

"Well," Molly said, a guilty look quickly spreading across her face. She rolled off the table and grabbed her small purse, sliding her panties off as well. A second later, she had a condom out and unwrapped.

"You dog!" I smiled, more relieved than I'd ever been.

Molly shrugged, embarrassed, then unrolled the slick latex down the length of my rod-stiff cock. I was about to lead her back to the couch, but she stopped me.

"I like the table." Her adorable face crinkled to one side.

"You freak you." I swept her up and kissed her some more. If nothing else, I could never get tired of just kissing her.

I laid her back down on the table and pressed my fat cock over her pussy. Her hanging legs immediately tightened as excitement rippled through her. I brushed the hair out of her face to get a better look at her beautiful dark eyes.

The thought of owning every part of her sent a hungry shiver through me, my nerve endings vibrating with anticipation. Her eyes smiled, knowing the effect she had on me. She'd always had power over my heart.

I grabbed her hips and slid them toward me. The table groaned angrily at the motion. She spread her knees wider, and I rubbed a thumb against her soaking wet lips. My cock flexed and jumped at the sight of her pussy spread and ready.

My cock aching, I slowly pushed my fat head down her engorged clit and into her wet opening. She rolled her shoulders back and moaned loudly as I filled her up. Frenzied waves of lightning rocketed through both of us.

This was finally happening!

I slid a hand over her breast and squeezed as I gently thrust inside of her. She clamped a hand over mine and forced me to grip her tighter. Her nipples were hardened dusky pebbles. I lowered myself over her, overcome by the urge to feel her nubs across my tongue.

I split her inner walls apart, letting them crush my cock as I buried myself in deep. My cock pulsed with every hot, wet inch I pushed into her. Her breath fluttered when I flexed, my cock finally basing out.

"Jesus," Molly said once she caught her breath.

Then I started fucking her.

My brain melted, and all I could see was her. It didn't matter if my eyes were open or shut. Her tight, soaked cunt crushed me as I slowly impaled her. Everything else in the room faded away. It was just the two of us and the long overdue joy of primal, sweaty love. I was a slave to her, and she to me.

For a few hours on a lonely Thursday evening, everything was finally right in the world.

We fucked slow and gentle at first. Then, as our passion edged closer to peaking, the intensity was amped up. I flipped her over onto her stomach, and she ground her ass into my hips.

I noticed a small Black Chains MC tattoo on her lower back that was halfway through the process of being removed. My head started to drift to darker things when Molly screamed out my name.

Immediately, I was back in my body and out of my head. Hearing her sultry voice call for me and no one else took all my restraint not to explode my condom like a carnival balloon. This was heaven, and her body shattered every vivid fantasy of her I'd ever had.

The wood whined, and my balls slapped her ass with each of our impacts. My hips moved with machine-like rhythm and intensity. I was fully lost in the pleasure of her sweet, sweet pussy. I couldn't get enough of her body.

"Yes!" Molly whimpered, mashing her ass tightly against my hips. The little explosions that ran through her set me off too.

We came together, hard and as one. Our heartbeats and breathing fell in sync with one another. The adrenaline spike I felt started in her body then coursed through mine. We were so close together, so in tune with each other, that it felt like we were the same person.

I'd never felt anything like it before.

And then when it was all over, we collapsed onto the table, lying next to each other. We were filthy, naked, and, for the first time in a long time, *fully satisfied.*

I was jonesing for a cigarette, but looking over at Molly all sweaty, naked, and exhausted… I thought I found something more addictive than smokes.

Some time later, we'd cleaned up and found ourselves on the couch looking through old photos of us on her phone. We stayed naked save for her putting her panties back on and me finding a pair of clean boxers to wear. It was the most domestic thing I'd done in years, and it staggered me how *normal* it felt.

It was like my arms were made just to hold her.

"Are you all right?" I asked. Thoughts of the faded

MC tattoo on her back buzzed around my head like an angry hornet on a hot day. Seeing her get slapped to the ground was its occasional sting.

"Better than all right." Molly still had sex in her voice.

I kissed her, smiling. It was a perfect moment—her and I on the couch, our bodies intertwined, reminiscing about past experiences. I wished I could tattoo this image of her on the inside of my eyelids so I'd never forget even the tiniest detail.

"I mean you and Jason." I paused, watching the moment shatter with the mention of her ex-husband's name. "I don't need the details." I already felt enough like a hypocrite. "I just need to know if he's going to hurt you."

"Jason…." Molly sat up and leaned away from me. Without the warmth of her bare olive skin, I felt cold. It had nothing to do with temperature; it felt like a part of me was being forcibly removed. I wasn't ready to let her go yet.

Molly adjusted her glasses and pulled the corner of her lips slightly to one side of her face. She looked pensive and a little sad. I hated seeing that on her.

"He'd tried courting me for years after you disappeared, but I always turned him down. Then when Matt died in the car accident, he was there for me when I needed someone."

Every word she said was a knife slicing across my skin, but I said nothing. I deserved to feel every ounce of her pain. Leaving might've been out of my control, but I should've come back so much earlier.

"Jason was a good guy once. He really was. For over a year, we were happy." Molly tucked a lock of hair behind her ear. "Happy enough anyway."

"What happened? Why did you leave him?"

"It was that fucking club." Her expression went from sadness to anger. "When he joined the Black Chains, I was supportive. I thought it would be good for him to belong to a brotherhood, even if they were bikers. I even let them tattoo their stupid logo on my back. So stupid…."

"We don't have to talk about this if—" I hated putting her through old pain.

"No, it's fine. I…." Molly pushed the air in her lungs out in one burst. "I need to talk to someone about this. I heard some of the other *old ladies* talking about what actually happened on the weekend-long rides they went on. Finally I paid one of the younger girls to take pictures when I wasn't around, and it was all perfectly clear."

"He was cheating on you?"

"That and doing drugs. I think the worst part of it was all the lies. 'My bike broke down; I need to spend the night.' 'Don't wait up, babe. I've gotta help with some club business.' It just got real bad real quick."

"Why not go to the police? Get a restraining order or have him arrested?"

"Who do you think is in the club with him?"

"Shit...."

"They're not all bad guys," Molly was quick to add. "Most of them are really decent in fact."

"But a brotherhood's still a brotherhood." I ran my hands over my head, smoothing my hair back. I'd gotten my answer. I was going to have to deal with Cannonball. "Hey," I said, lightening the mood, "Dad's having Richard and me over for dinner this Saturday. Having you there would definitely keep me sane."

"I don't know." Molly peeled her bottom lip back, exposing some teeth. She looked a little apprehensive. "It's been a long time. I can't even remember the last time I was there."

"I remember. You let me get to second base," I said mischievously. Molly smiled and shoved me. "But seriously, I know he'd love to see you."

"I'll think about it." Molly crawled toward me, and I grabbed her.

I wanted to hold onto her and this moment for as long as possible, because if I knew one thing about the King family, it was that that dinner was going to be a fucking nightmare.

CHAPTER 17

Richard

"Go ahead," I said carefully, driving up my father's long driveway. My cell was hooked up to the car's speakers with Bluetooth. Madison sat silently next to me.

"It's me," Lucas said. "I want to call a truce for the night."

"A truce?" Hearing his voice put me a little on edge. Lucas was more vindictive than I was; there was no way he was going to let me get away with canceling his show. These past two weeks, I'd kept my guard up and waited for a blow that never came.

I had no intention of sinking to his level, especially at our father's estate while he was sick. The skeptical side of me wondered if he'd even keep any bargain we made.

"You play nice. I play nice. We smile, humor the old man, and part ways." The audio was crisp enough to pick up notes of fatigue in his voice.

Was he as exhausted with this war as I was?

I'd never play my hand and ask him directly, of course. The fight went out of me when I saw Gloria hurt. My mind lingered on that girl far more than it should have. I was excellent at putting my feelings in little boxes and discarding them. That was the essence of good business.

So why couldn't I do that with her?

I glanced at Madison when we stopped near the valet. She was intently touching up her makeup in a small mirror she carried with her. She appeared not to be listening to our call, but I knew better.

She's a politician's daughter with aspirations of following in her father's footsteps, I reminded myself. *Some battles are fought in the boardroom, while others are fought casually everywhere else.*

Necessary evils. Madison felt like the wrong train headed in the right direction.

I took my phone out of a nook in the dashboard and hesitated. Was it me? Was I being paranoid?

Madison was going to be the mother of my child, I needed to start trusting her. I took the phone off speakerphone. The fact that I couldn't trust her made me worried about the man I was becoming.

Was I always on my guard around Gloria?

"Play nice, how?" I asked.

"Y'know when we were young and we used to pretend to be brothers?" Lucas said. I felt a stab of pain deep inside somewhere. For many years, he *was* my best friend. We used to be extremely close. It truly was a shame it had come to this.

How did we drift so far apart?

"No fucking the other over," Lucas continued. There was no sharpness to his voice. This wasn't a threat of mutually assured destruction. It almost sounded like he was asking me, without asking me. "And no discussing the inheritance."

"That's fair." I sighed, suddenly feeling tired myself. "For Dad's sake…."

There was a long empty space at the end of the phone call where a *thank you* or a *goodbye* would've gone. Neither of us said anything, but it felt important that that space was even there.

My door was opened for me by the valet, and I, in turn, opened the door for Madison, then helped her out of the car.

She wore a pale, blush, backless gown with jewel embellishments that accentuated her curves and even made them glow in certain light. Her golden hair was done up in a neat French twist, interwoven with white, beaded accents. Her short train lightly swept the pavement but was kept hovering about an inch from the ground by her tall stiletto heels when she stood up.

Madison simply looked incredible.

"Ready, darling?" she asked, confidently.

"Not even a little." I smiled, taking her arm, then led her inside.

The house was fully staffed tonight, and it had a warmth I hadn't seen the last few times I visited. I'd have liked to see him every day, but Dad abhorred appearing weak. Despite his sudden worldview change, some old habits died hard.

A butler took our coats and led us to the sitting room. The fireplace was lit, and classical music played softly in the background.

"It's good to be home, isn't it?" Madison asked, noticing my smile.

It was, but that wasn't why I was smiling. I thought of Gloria on my arm and her changing the classical music to the thrashy, punk rock New York Dolls. She'd turn to me and say, *"There, isn't that way better?"*

"Richard, my boy!" Dad said, from behind me. When I turned around, my heart sank. He rolled forward in an electric wheelchair. There was an IV stand integrated into it, so as to be as minimally intrusive as possible. Dad wore a fine tux, but his lap and legs were covered by a blanket.

He looked scarily thin.

There was a lot of effort put into tonight's dinner to make things appear as normal as possible. Knowing how much effort was needed to keep up that illusion broke my heart.

"Hey there, young man." I smiled weakly, trying to keep the worry and fear from my voice. I reached down and hugged him. "It's good to see you, Dad."

I introduced Madison.

"Pleasure, miss." He shook Madison's hand, then pointed to the hospital band on his wrist. "Please don't mind the bracelet. It's so the doctors remember my blood type."

My eyes narrowed skeptically.

"What blood type are you?" Madison asked.

"Red," he said with a wink, then let go of her hand. Madison laughed as if the joke was genuinely amusing.

I knew it. I groaned, but seeing him maintain his corny sense of humor lifted the sense of dread I felt inside. Maybe it only looked worse than it was. It was a lie, I knew, but at least it was a comforting one.

Shortly thereafter, Lucas showed up with Molly and greeted my father.

Molly's dress was a modest, green, strapless gown. Her dark hair hung in layered waves about her shoulders. She looked as pretty as when those two had dated in high school, except now she was all grown up. The only thing that looked out of place was a charm bracelet she wore on her wrist.

"Molly, you look radiant," I said, kissing her on the cheek. While Molly's back was turned, Madison looked the girl over with the critical stare of a hated rival. Then, like a light switch, she turned on her practiced smile when I introduced her.

There was no jealousy in Madison's initial expression. She wasn't the kind of girl that cared about that sort of thing. She'd even written an allowance for extramarital lovers into the proposal.

No, Molly was simply some debris on Madison's road to victory, which needed to be quietly and efficiently removed.

I'd have to watch that. The last thing I wanted was for a girl like Molly to be hurt in any way.

"Richard." Lucas extended a stiff hand. Lucas had his dirty blond hair pulled back and his light beard neatly kempt. He wore *most* of an off-the-rack suit, missing only the tie. Despite the top button of his shirt being undone, he'd cleaned up well.

"Hello, Lucas." We shook hands briskly, yet firmly. It wasn't until I saw Lucas and Molly together that I realized he might *actually win* this competition. I chided myself for still thinking of Gloria. That raven-haired beauty had burrowed into my heart and weakened my resolve. I needed to get her out of my head if I had any chance of coming out on top.

The battlefield may have changed, but this was still war.

Not tonight, I reminded myself of the call we had earlier. *There'll be no bloodshed tonight.*

For the next hour, Lucas and I mostly avoided one another. We alternated between talking with Dad—who downplayed the severity of his health—and talking with the nurse, who tried her best to soften the blow of the harsh reality. The cancer was spreading as fast as they could kill it.

Dad coughed a sharp raspy sound that dragged on far longer than anyone in the room was comfortable with.

At best, Dad had a few months left to live.

It didn't matter who won. He'd never live long enough to see a grandchild.

I glanced over at Lucas while he talked with the nurse. I watched him go through all the same emotions when he heard the news. Finally, he looked back at me, his eyes glossy and full of pain. We shared the same useless anger and sense of overwhelming futility.

What the fuck is the point?

When approached privately, Dad had outright refused to answer questions about the inheritance competition. "It's how it needs to be" was all he'd say before changing the subject.

It would've been one thing if he hated us and wanted us to suffer, but that was never the case. We might not have been as tightly knit as families you'd see on TV, but there was no denying that Lucas and I were loved. Why else would Dad have adopted Lucas? He tried so hard to bring us together after Mom died, but by then the damage between Lucas and I was done.

Why spend the twilight of his life undoing everything? Why rip the family even further apart with this damn competition?

Despite Dad's bad jokes, it was apparent that the exertion of appearing as if nothing was wrong was taking its toll on the old man. He began slouching in his chair and had trouble following conversations. If he was a phone's battery, he'd be flashing red.

The evening looked to be at its bleakest. I didn't know if he was going to make it to dinner. Then, out of nowhere, a series of smooth notes were played on the grand piano in the next room over.

There was no denying Molly was a little out of practice, at least at first. Or it might've been the piano that was rusty; it hadn't felt the warm touch of skilled fingers since Mom died. That didn't matter to Dad, his weathered, old face brightened right up at the sound. The classical music was turned off to make way for the Chopin and Bach that Molly played. And like a great migration, we all made our way over to watch.

Lucas leaned on the piano, propping himself up on his elbows to watch her play. It was the same thing he used to do whenever Mom asked her to play.

"Maggie…," Dad said, wheeling himself next to me. He patted me gently on my lower back. The music made him look ten years younger than a few minutes ago. His eyes were floating, every keystroke brought him a little closer to openly weeping. "She sounds just like your mother, doesn't she?"

"Yeah, Dad." I placed a hand on his shoulder.

In that moment, I desperately wanted to tell him, "*Everything's going to be all right, don't worry.*"

But I stayed silent. I was too afraid to hear the words out loud, knowing them to be just another happy lie.

Dad had dried the tears that ran down his cheeks as

Molly wrapped up the last of the half a dozen songs she could still remember. The chef entered, whispered something to Dad, then disappeared from the room.

"Beautiful! Thank you, my dear." Dad hugged Molly, whose light blush reddened her olive cheeks. "Maggie would've been so proud of you."

Molly smiled, fighting back tears of her own, and hugged him again.

"Now," he declared, charged back up by the music. "I don't know about any of you, but that long drive down memory lane dropped me off in Hungary." Lucas and I both groaned at the bad joke in perfect unison. "Dinner is served!"

CHAPTER 18

Lucas

I shoved my mostly empty plate away, feeling ready to explode. Five helpings was one too many.

Molly shot me an I-told-you-so look. She asked me if I was trying to set a world record around the fourth heaping plate. I didn't want to tell her I was casually trying to beat Richard… but that was only because he was casually trying to beat me.

"You can look at me any way you want." I raised both my arms and flexed. "Muscles like these don't grow on trees." Then I leaned in and proudly whispered, "After the workout we had earlier today, I needed my protein."

I wasn't sure who won the informal eating contest, but either way it was good to just be silly again. If it wasn't for Richard's date—the woman who looked like someone's press secretary—it would've felt like a real family dinner.

Dinner was a holy time in our house while Mom was alive. Mom and Dad used to cook dinner, and we were forced to clean the dishes. They said it built character to clean up after ourselves. I thought it was bullshit.

What's the point of making all that money if you can't pay people to do stuff for you?

They were right, of course. Looking back, it always seemed like they were right; we were just too young and spoiled to see that at the time.

Like the good little boys we were, Richard and I started clearing the plates. It was only when I grabbed Dad's that I saw how little he'd actually eaten. He'd apparently only been moving the food around as we all made strained but pleasant-enough conversation.

"I had a big lunch," Dad said, reassuringly. He saw that the lie didn't ease the worried look on my face because he patted my arm and changed the subject. "Just load them into the dishwasher. I think you boys have mastered the fine art of washing dishes by now."

"I think I might need a refresher." I gave him a half smile. "If it's worth doing once…."

"It's worth doing a thousand times," Richard said, breezing past us with full arms.

Dad just laughed, having been beaten to finish his favorite phase. Dad began softly interrogating Molly and Madison, asking them about their lives. Richard and I escaped to the kitchen to wash dishes and wrap and put away leftovers.

"You know I won, right?" Richard said with an easy grin. His jacket was off and sleeves were rolled up as he pulled plastic wrap over a casserole dish.

I froze as warm tap water steadily ran over my hands and the cup I was washing. What did he mean "won"? *Won* won? Is the plastic anchorwoman in there actually pregnant?

Then it dawned on me that I never even told Molly about the clause in the inheritance. I wasn't intentionally keeping that from her. We *just* got back together; I wanted to make sure we were good *first* before I dropped something that heavy on her.

"Hi, Molly, I haven't seen you in a decade. I've never stopped loving you. I need to get you pregnant ASAP." In no universe did those three fucking sentences make it into the same paragraph.

Hell, I couldn't even imagine them in the same book.

"I ate six," Richard said, brimming with smugness.

I exhaled hard and steadied myself. *Thank, Christ!* He wasn't talking about the inheritance.

"Bullshit, you did. A lone buttered roll doth not a plate maketh," I did my best Shakespeare impression. "My last plate piled high with salad."

"Salad? No." He scoffed. "There weren't any tomatoes, onions, carrots…. Did you even have dressing?" He paused, trying to remember. "No jury in the country would call that a salad. Besides, you didn't even finish it."

We continued to argue the legality of produce for a lot longer than should've been possible. Eventually, without any clear winner, the argument fizzled away like it always used to. There wasn't any mention of the elephant in the room that caused the massive rift between us. We kept everything surprisingly light.

Standing here with my brother like that after so long was surreal. Nothing was forgiven. The truce was only for the night, but I started wondering if we could just talk this whole thing out like sensible adults, like brothers.

"What happened to the black-haired girl you left your party with?" I asked idly, drying my hands with a bright red hand towel.

"It didn't work out." He paused, then continued as if he was reassuring himself rather than explaining anything to me. "Madison is a better fit. We have similar goals."

Why the fuck would you want a social chameleon like her? Surprisingly, I held my tongue. It wasn't something I probably would've done yesterday. Nevertheless, I didn't like that woman, and it wasn't just because she was with Richard.

I didn't like her fake smile or her precise laugh. I didn't like the way I felt her eyes dissecting me for exploitable weakness while I wasn't looking. Madison didn't have strong opinions, and she didn't make waves. I could talk to her for days and have no fucking idea who she was.

I didn't like the thought of someone like that with my brother.

"That's a shame." I threw the towel at him, which he caught easily. He proceeded to neatly fold it then put it away. "She looked like she was a free spirit. That would've been good for you. What was her name?"

"Gloria," he said, before I even finished the question. Her name was ready in his mind, *too* ready. I looked hard at him.

Did he actually care for Gloria?

Richard had the same look of longing in his eyes that I had when I was seriously missing Molly.

Holy shit… he does care for her!

He was only with Madison because of the inheritance. Gloria probably didn't want kids, and Madison… she seemed like the kind of person who wanted only whatever would get her ahead.

Fuck. I actually felt sorry for the guy. I couldn't remember Richard ever finding a girl he had a real connection with. He'd been with a lot of girls, sure, but they were just flings, nothing serious.

And now he went and fell in love just to throw it away so he could win a competition.

All these years I thought he was the smart one….

After that busted show at the Family Room, once the cops and EMTs cleared me to leave, I had a realization. I wasn't going to win the bet. I wasn't going to win because I knew I would never be happy with anyone else but Molly. I couldn't just knock some girl up and hope for the best.

If I didn't have *her*, then I didn't have anything worth fighting for.

"Hey, man." I sighed. Against my better judgment, I decided to extend an olive branch. "We really haven't talked about this whole inheritance thing."

"Wasn't that why you called me earlier, so we *wouldn't* discuss it?"

"I just didn't want to argue about it in front of Dad. He's got a lot going on; he doesn't need to deal with that shit too."

Richard crossed his arms and nodded gravely. "What about the inheritance?"

"This whole thing is fucking crazy. Maybe we can talk this over and come up with another solution."

The sound of shattering glass rang out before Richard could answer. We immediately shelved the conversation and rushed back into the dining room. Thoughts of Dad falling out of his chair or cutting himself or a million other things raced through my mind.

Fortunately, it wasn't Dad. He wasn't in the room at all. He'd probably been taken by the nurse to the bathroom or to take medicine.

Madison sat calmly in her chair, wearing an expression of slight embarrassment. It was the look someone had when they accidentally spoiled a surprise party on purpose. And Molly?

Molly. Was. Pissed.

Molly stepped over the broken wine glass at her feet and stormed over to me.

"What happened? Is everything—" The words were slapped out of my mouth.

"You fucking asshole!" Molly didn't exactly scream the words, but her voice and pitch gradually rose to the point that if she said anything more it would be said at the top of her lungs.

Molly tore off the bracelet I'd given her and dropped it like it burned her hand.

"Molly…."

"Y'know, this time I really thought it was going to be different. I actually thought you came back for me. How fucking stupid am I, huh?" Molly shoved me, the tears rolling down her cheeks ruining her mascara.

With one look of utter betrayal, I felt my whole world crumbling apart like a sandcastle under a heavy boot.

Oh no….

I waited too long. Why could I not stop fucking things up!

"All of this was just to beat Richard?" Molly went to slap me again but couldn't muster the hatred through all that sadness. "Goddamn you, Luke."

When she left, I lurched forward as if she had a thread wrapped around my heart. Once she was far enough away, the imaginary line snapped taught and it ripped my heart right out of my chest.

I was too stunned to move, to think, to *breathe*. After everything that happened, could it really end this way?

"Luke, I…," Richard started, then stopped, not able to find the words he was looking for.

The sound of his voice was like a cheese grater on my soul. I turned to face my *half brother* with eyes on fire. I mirrored Molly's feelings of betrayal and anger. I was a fool for not telling her the truth when I had the chance, but I was a bigger fool for trusting Richard not to fuck me over when he had the chance.

"We had a truce, you motherfucker!" I didn't even realize I hit him until he was bleeding on the floor. He wasn't knocked out or anything. I cocked my fist to hit him again, but he didn't raise his arms in defense. Why would he?

It wouldn't matter if I beat him to a pulp. He was a ruthless, cutthroat businessman, and he'd already got what he wanted.

He'd already won.

"For a second there…," I said, unclenching my hands and letting my arms lower to my sides. "I almost thought you were my brother."

I left the happy couple to their hollow victory and chased after Molly. She'd have already asked one of the valets to drive her home, but I had to at least try to reach her. Try to apologize. Anything!

"What?" I heard Madison ask Richard in her reptilian voice right before I rounded the corner that would take me out of the house. "You wanted to win, didn't you?"

CHAPTER 19

Richard

It was barely daybreak, and Black Rocket Records was busier than I'd ever seen, but not with customers, although they were there too. Half the store bustled about urgently with renovations. Was this all for that band's album release concert?

The executive side of me quickly calculated the cost of the manpower, the materials, and the temporary loss of revenue due to the construction. This wasn't something a small store could afford easily. A pit formed in my stomach.

If this concert didn't go exactly as planned, the Rocket might not be able to make its next bank payment. That's when bad things started happening.

I spotted Gloria immediately. She was barking orders at half a dozen workers nearly twice her size.

Gloria wore a black, ragged-top T-shirt, and ripped jeans. She was sweaty from coordinating, moving things, and also taking care of customers that were brave enough to enter.

Where was Judy in all this?

I walked in, idly rubbing my silver cufflinks. The last few weeks had been an avalanche of mistakes, and I was tumbling hard down the wrong path.

I canceled my engagement with Madison the night of the dinner. She unsurprisingly threatened legal action for a breach of our agreement. Fortunately, nothing was signed yet, so she didn't have a leg to stand on.

In a lot of ways, walking into that coffee shop felt like I was back at square one. I had just arrived to town with no attachments and was looking to accomplish a goal. That goal had changed though. It wasn't about the inheritance anymore.

It was about Gloria.

This time I was going to do it all the right way.

"Look what the cat dragged in." Gloria wiped the sweat from her eyes with the back of her arm. Her shock of black hair was both matted to the side of her face and also stuck up at random angles.

"Must've been a big cat," I replied, with a half smirk. The joke went over like a lead balloon. Gloria wasn't pleased to see me.

"I don't have time for games." She swept a hand at the men working on the stage and rearranging the store to fit the coming crowd. "There's still a lot of shit that needs to be done before Friday."

I switched to plan B.

"I was going to bring flowers…." I held up the bottle of fine whiskey I'd brought for her. It was a bottle of Glenlivet vintage nineteen sixty-four. Only a hundred bottles were ever produced. It arrived from Ireland this morning. "But I figured this was more your speed."

"Yeah, thanks," Gloria said, unimpressed. She lifted a cardboard box full of extension cords and walked toward the stage. "Leave it behind the bar."

I frowned, snatching the box out of her arms with one hand. Gloria sighed, realizing that I wasn't going to let her carry it while I was standing here, then pointed to the stage. One of the workers grabbed the box when I got close.

"Let me help." I set the bottle of expensive whiskey on the shelf beneath the cash register. Walking back to her, I took my jacket off and tossed it on a nearby chair. "Looks like you could use an extra hand."

"I don't want you to wreck your thousand-dollar loafers." She smiled bitterly and without humor. Her icy tone stopped me from rolling up my second sleeve.

"Where's Judy?" I asked, keeping the conversation light. I was trying to create the right atmosphere for an apology. It didn't matter how sorry I was; if she wasn't ready to hear it, then it would just fall on deaf ears.

"Probably draining the rest of our fucking bank account to pay for all this," Gloria muttered under her breath. Then in a louder voice she said, "I don't know.

Not here. Which is exactly where *you* should be."

"Wait." I gritted my teeth; this wasn't how I anticipated this meeting would go. "About that letter—"

"That *letter* was awfully clear. You don't want to be with me. I get it. I'm sure you and Business Barbie will make a great couple." Gloria left to help a customer.

She poured the girl a coffee, glanced over at me, then asked to see the girl's ID. Confused, the college girl riffled through her satchel and eventually produced a driver's license. Gloria carefully read it, then gifted the girl a twenty-five-thousand-dollar bottle of liquor. The girl thanked Gloria with a wide but still confused smile, then went off to the self-service station.

She turned back toward me with a raised eyebrow and a look that said, *You can't buy my affection.*

Gloria was serving a small line of customers when I walked over. I wondered how she was going to spite me now that she was out of gifts to give away. In between pouring cups of coffee and taking payment from people, she asked me, "Can't you see that I'm busy?"

"Extremely so."

"So tell me, Richard…." She slapped the cup down on the glass counter, forcing the customer back a step to avoid hot splashing liquid. Gloria turned to me with a mix of anger and hurt floating in her stormy gray eyes. "What is it you want from me?"

I finally understood how Lucas felt when he'd

lost Molly.

I ran over this conversation in my head hundreds of times. I broke it down into sections, planned it, and practiced it. Realizing I wasn't going to get the right atmosphere for it, I went for my apology anyway.

All my practiced lines suddenly felt canned and artificial. They all came from the heart, but they weren't as passionate as they needed to be. I let them dissolve in my mind and went with the only thing that actually felt honest.

"I'm sorry."

Gloria's stone expression softened at the sincerity in my words, but that only lasted for a moment. Her resolve hardened immediately.

"I don't care," she said. "I want you to go."

It was hard for me to wrap my head around her words. They were so... final. There wasn't room for negotiation or a better offer. Suddenly, it hit me. For the first time in my life, I'd committed myself to something and I *failed.* That pit in my stomach became a wide chasm.

I wasn't going to win this one.

I wasn't going to win *her.*

Defeated, I walked out of Black Rocket Records. I hadn't even bothered to grab my jacket. It didn't matter.

"Sir?" James, my driver, asked seeing the disappointment that bore heavy lines on my face. He shook his head while opening the car door for me, then corrected himself. "Is everything all right, *Richard?*"

It was a surprise he remembered our earlier conversations about titles and names. I hadn't requested his services since the day he first brought me here. I didn't know what to tell him, so I didn't tell him anything.

No, everything is not all right.

For a long time, we simply idled in the car parked by the side of the road. He'd asked me where I wanted to go, but again I couldn't answer.

I wasn't the kind of man who was ever racked by indecision or hesitation. Whether it was the right call or even occasionally the wrong call, I'd always been able to make it quickly and decisively.

"Take me to my jet," I said at length. "I'm done with Caldwell Hope."

"Would you like anything from your apartment packed for you?"

"No," I said gravely. The full weight of my failure in all things was pushing me into the back seat. Soon I'd disappear into the folds of leather and never be seen again. "There's nothing left for me here."

I'd failed Gloria.

I'd failed my father.

I'd even found a way to fail Lucas.

So what? Dad's voice said in the back of my mind. I imagined his voice shrugging indifferently somehow. *It is only the last failure that mattered; the one that stopped you from trying again.*

I dwelled on those words as we drove in silence.

I thought about the whole cryptic conversation we had that first day as we overlooked the town. We talked for such a long time, yet so much went unsaid.

My ringing phone jolted me from memory.

"Richard speaking," I said, distractedly. Part of me was still sitting on the bench behind my father's estate, listening to him talk.

"Hi, Richard. This is Jackie, your father's nurse. I'm afraid I have some terrible news—"

My heart sank like a stone in a pond.

"I'll be right there," I said. I knew what she was going to tell me, but I didn't want her to say the awful, final words out loud.

Your father is dead.

CHAPTER 20

"Lucas?" a familiar voice in the hallway of my apartment called out.

I lay on the floor near the couch, plucking at my guitar. Through the haze of dead beer, every once in a while I could smell Molly's perfume. It racked me with pain to know what I'd lost. Every time one of those dark thoughts threatened to break me, I played faster and yelled out the lyrics I had. The song still wasn't done.

Why couldn't I finish this fucking song?

I'd been at it for days now, and I couldn't figure the damn thing out! Molly's song needed another verse and an outro, but every time I wrote one it fucked with something else!

It was driving me crazy. I didn't sleep. I didn't eat. I

just wrote and played. Writer's block had crippled me after the dinner at my father's place. I tried all week to explain, but Molly wouldn't see me or return my calls.

After that, I locked myself in this room and threw away the key.

That's why I needed to finish her song. I knew— *knew*—if I could figure it out, then everything between us would work out too. It had to....

"Lucas," the man repeated. "Are you home?"

The poet in me poured over all the other meanings of that phrase.

"Luke's not home." Caldwell Hope wasn't my home anymore. It's just another place I used to live.

"Oh good, you're here." Richard stepped over the cardboard cases long since emptied of beer. He wore a fine charcoal suit and had a tray of food in his hands.

After what he did, he was the last person I wanted to see.

"No one invited you!" I threw the nearest thing I could reach. He didn't even have to dodge; the empty beer bottle flew wildly off course and shattered against a wall nowhere near him.

"No one mopes quite like a rock star." Richard cleared a space on the kitchen counter and put the food down.

"The fuck do you want, Dick?"

"I got a call from management. They were worried that you hadn't been eating and some of the guests have been complaining about loud crashes in the middle of the night."

"No one trashes a hotel room like a *rock star* either."
I raised my warm bottle of beer, then took a sip

"You're already drinking?" Richard at least tried to
mask his disapproval this time, although I could still
hear it in his voice. "It's eight in the morning."

"Eight a.m. to you maybe." I finished the bottle, laid
it on its side, then rolled it away. Time didn't matter
to me. I had all the time in the world to fuck up now.
"How'd you even get in?"

"I told you, management called me over. They
probably thought you were dead and didn't want to be
the ones to stumble across your body."

"Well, I'm alive." I spread my arms out. "Now get
the fuck out."

Richard sighed and unbuttoned his jacket so he
could sit in a chair easily. "I'm not here just for that."

"Dad's dead, isn't he?" The thought sobered me up
immediately.

Richard looked down and said nothing. That's
when I noticed his red-rimmed eyes. He didn't need to
answer; I knew it was true.

"When?" Nausea bubbled up my throat.

"A few hours ago. He just never woke up."

I didn't know if it was from the beer or what, but
I wasn't as destroyed as I thought I'd be hearing the
news. I'd spent so much time pushing thoughts of his
health out of my head that I had never prepared myself
for when it actually happened.

I felt numb.

"I'll go get changed." I got up and left the room. I even made it all the way to the bathroom before I vomited my guts out into the toilet. It was mostly booze, and it smelled awful.

I took a long shower, waiting for the tears to come. They never did. The fact that he wasn't my biological parent didn't mean a damn thing to me. He was my *real* father, and I loved him. That's what bothered me the most.

Was I so broken that I couldn't even cry for the death of a loved one?

CHAPTER 21

The rest of the day was a painful circus of bullshit.

Richard and I got some food to help me sober up, then started making the arrangements.

I quickly discovered that I hated the whole system of taking care of a dead family member. Between the medical examiner, the funeral director, getting the death certificate, and planning the wake, there was no time to grieve.

How did they expect anyone to do all this?

It was like trying to plan a birthday party after just getting stabbed in the heart. The whole thing was fucking insane!

At the end of the day—that felt like a month—Richard and I drank beers in Dad's garage. He sat in the Aston Martin, and I sat next to him in the nineteen sixty-six Shelby Cobra. The tops were down in each car, making it easy to talk to one another.

"What a fucking zoo," Richard said, popping the top on a cold beer.

I did a double take at him. Richard never swore. That polished, professional exterior was finally breaking down enough that someone might mistake him for an actual person.

"Is what's her face coming to the funeral?" We decided to keep the wake small and private. Family was flying in from all over the world. The rest of the week was going to be hell. Richard gave me a questioning look that needed clarification. "Uh... Madeline? You know the one who looked like the blonde Terminator robot from that movie."

"Madi*son*." Richard chuckled. "No, she's long gone."

"Good. I didn't like her. You really aught to call the dark-haired girl though. You smiled more while you were with her."

"So people tell me…." He blew out his air, shaking his head, then took another sip. "That's over too. You talk to Molly?"

"She won't see me either." I pressed the perspiring can into my forehead, letting the condensation cool my skin. It was a balmy, awful night, and I still felt like shit from the week-long bender. "We're really bad at this whole falling-in-love thing."

"Amen to that." Richard tipped his beer slightly in a mock toast.

"I didn't knock anyone up." I turned to him and asked, "You?"

"Nope. I have no idea what's going to happen to his inheritance now that he's gone. My lawyers are looking over the will, but with the way he was acting these past few months, it's anyone's guess."

"If there's a historical society of puns and bad jokes," I said flippantly, "he probably donated it all to them."

Richard laughed.

We reminisced about old funny memories involving our parents and even some of the hard ones. Most of it was positive though, and talking to Richard felt good. For the first time in a long time, we were completely on equal footing. We were two parentless children sharing our loss with one another.

It was a very brotherly thing to do.

Some time passed, and a familiar buzzed feeling washed over me. It helped me draw up the courage to ask something I never thought I would.

"Why did you hate me so much?"

"I never hated you, Lucas. If anything, I was jealous."

"Jealous?" I chuckled, getting caught by surprise. "What the fuck for? I'm not even biologically a King."

"That never mattered to me. We were close long before either of us knew about your adoption. I was jealous of how easily you figured things out."

"You're crazy. You got way better grades than me."

"That's only because you didn't try. Remember that catapult I made for science class?"

"The one that exploded?" I laughed, remembering the look on his teacher's face when it hurled the rubber band ball in the opposite direction, then fell apart like in an old cartoon.

"Yup. Once we found all the pieces, you had that thing reassembled in no time. When we tried it again, it doubled the distance of any other catapult. I still have the first-place ribbon somewhere.

"My point is, had you just focused your natural talents, you'd have been a force to be reckoned with. You could've done great things for the family company."

"I always loved the family, even during the dark times when I had to go live with the Morenas. I just couldn't do the grad school and college thing, man. My passion wasn't in any of it. I wasn't cut out for a life of business."

"That's why you didn't accept the partnership offer at my company when you left the Morenas." It slowly started to dawn on him. "Dad thought the deal had voided years earlier, so that day they came knocking took us all by surprise."

"I should've handled that better, I'm sorry," I said, finally seeing how poorly I handled the whole situation back in the day. I'd basically told Richard to go fuck himself. "I didn't mean to blow you off like that. I was still all fucked up from the deal Dad made to adopt me.

I guess I wasn't feeling much like a part of the family at the time.

"You were the golden son—smart, ruthless, and always in a rush. You followed perfectly in Dad's footsteps, the quintessential, high-powered corporate executive. You were exactly what our father wanted an ideal son to be."

My voice cracked at several parts, the words I said raking the bottom of my very soul. I usually wore my emotions on my sleeve, but this shit was all buried down deep. In an already emotional day, this stuff was hard to get out.

"I was suddenly the one that didn't fit in," I finished, looking away. Facing anyone after admitting all that was tough, let alone the man I hated for years.

Richard got out of his car and sat next to me in the Shelby. He opened a beer and gave it to me.

"It didn't matter who your real father was. As far as we were all concerned, you were always one of us." Richard let the words float in the air for a long while.

What did I say to that?

With the news of what happened to Dad and the shit show that was literally everything else in my life, I honestly didn't know how to feel. After I found out I was adopted, I put up these barriers between me and the rest of the family. It was like I was keeping them all at arm's reach so I wouldn't get hurt again.

"For as much of a pain in the ass as you are, you're always going to be my little brother." Richard put his arm around my shoulders and hugged me.

I never dreamed Richard and I would have a heart-to-heart, we were just so different…. I felt so heavy yet so light at the same time. Even through the sadness surrounding my dad's death, a massive burden had been lifted. I had my brother back.

I didn't have to keep it together any longer.

For several long minutes, the tough, in-charge King brothers wept like only those in mourning can. We lowered our guards and let ourselves openly cope with not only the grief of loss but also the realization that we were siblings that didn't have to hate each other.

We could choose a different path.

"We've been acting like real assholes, huh?" I was so tired of fucking things up and making things worse all the time. There had to be a way to fix things.

"It's the King way after all. If you ignore your problems, they'll probably go away."

"Or they'll blow up in your fucking face," I said. The sudden exhaustion of redlining these past few days hit me like a speeding train. I didn't know how much bonding I had left in me before I just passed out. I wouldn't leave just yet; this was all too important.

"I don't know why Dad put that clause in the inheritance, but he was right about one thing," I said.

"What's that?"

"He said we'd never be able to find better women in the world than the ones here."

"There are two women out there we can't live without." Richard nodded thoughtfully; then his eyes narrowed dangerously. I knew right away that an idea just popped into his head when he started rubbing his cufflinks. It was a habit he never outgrew. "I've got a new proposition for you."

I looked at him sideways. "Another competition?"

That's just what we needed....

"No," he said, waving his beer back and forth, shunning the idea. "Look where that's gotten us. I propose we work together and actually *help* each other."

"What about the inheritance?" This didn't seem like him at all. It was the opposite of pragmatism. Help the other get all the money?

"We don't even know if there is an inheritance anymore." He looked at me with hard blue eyes that were so similar to my own it was almost like looking into a mirror. "Can you honestly tell me that money is more important to you than getting Molly back?"

There wasn't any doubt in my mind. Molly was more important to me than all the money this world had to offer.

"What do you have in mind?"

CHAPTER 22

Richard

The school was brighter than I'd expected. I walked through the halls of Matt Baker Elementary, hands in my pockets, admiring how much work had been done. Lucas and I were homeschooled until about sixth grade; then both of us in turn were sent off to the best private school in the area.

I'd never met Molly's brother, Matthew Baker. Lucas and Molly were about three years younger than I was, and they were older than Matt by a few years. By all accounts, he was growing into a good man when his life was tragically cut short by a drunk driver. Both Molly and Matt had gone to Classical when they were children, so it was nice to see him memorialized in this way.

I'd only ever been here once, back when it was called

Classical. Large, cartoon images of brass instruments adorned the wall then. They, like everything else in the aging school, were timeworn, faded, and in desperate need of replacing.

Now the halls were painted with superheroes like Batman and Wonder Woman; they stood next to Aladdin, Elsa, and other Disney characters. Peering into the classrooms, I could see they were lined with vivid colors and were inviting. Everything was new and safe; all the computers were state of the art.

This was the best possible version of what this school could've been.

Dad had spoken in front of the graduating class one year, and I tagged along. He talked about the virtue of working hard and how important it was to be armed with knowledge. I could only remember one line of his speech. "The real world is a series of locked doors," he'd said. "School, and places like it, is where you find the keys."

It darkened my heart to think about how much of his wisdom I'd forgotten over the years.

It had been several days since the funeral.

It was a formal, bleak ordeal. It seemed like half the town had shown up at one point or another. Many people flew in from all over to pay their respects. There were speeches and songs; the mayor even named the intersection of Main Street and Marshall Long Avenue after him and Mom in honor of where they met.

The whole thing was intimate, sad, and wonderful

all at the same time. Dad was many things to many people.

I was just glad it was over. Things had gotten far more emotional than I was comfortable dealing with.

The bell rang out over the intercom, signifying the end of the school day; it was followed by a friendly female voice wishing everyone a nice afternoon and to remember to have their permission slips signed for the upcoming field trips.

Classroom doors swung open like a dam giving way, and a flood of children cascaded into the halls around me. The sereneness of the casual walk had been shattered by screaming, laughing, and even some singing.

Walking through the bright, oblivious elementary school halls was a nice change of pace from the sorrow-filled clouds that hung over my interactions with adults that knew my father. The children here didn't know or care about him; they were too busy living and playing.

I reached the open wood and glass doors of my destination. "Everything you're looking for," read the beautifully carved sign above the library's entrance.

I hoped the sign was right.

"Hello?" I asked, looking around the expansive library. It didn't just have books; it had graphic novels, an extensive computer lab, and even a small nook to take naps or read on the plush floor. It was larger than any other library of its kind, and it was far more inviting. If I were a kid, this would be where I spent all my free time.

"Just a moment please." Molly returned to the check-in desk with an armful of abandoned books that needed to get returned to their appropriate shelves. "Richard, hi," she said with surprised eyes. "How did you even get in?"

Molly's brown hair was drawn into a tight ponytail. She wore black dress pants, a layered, sleeveless, violet blouse, and bright blue glasses. The afternoon light revealed the dusting of freckles across her nose and cheeks.

I pressed my lips together, then shrugged in a modest gesture.

"*Right*. You're a King," Molly exhaled in a short, knowing burst. A crease in her lips made it resemble a smile. "Is there anywhere you can't go in this town?"

"They still won't let me into the women's roller derby locker room." I smiled.

"Somehow, I'm not so sure that's true." Molly shook her head, then gave me a big hug. Afterward, a look of worry raised her eyebrows. "I'm so sorry about your father. He was a great guy. How are you holding up?"

Molly had briefly appeared at the funeral to show her respects to the family. She'd even broken down a little when she hugged Lucas. For as much time as Molly spent at the house, she never really got to know my dad because he was always away on work.

Molly and my mom were much closer. She took Mom's death much harder.

"Thanks. We're getting by. It's a lot to adjust to, of course." I kept the conversation light. Doom and gloom wasn't why I was here. "He's not in any pain anymore. I hope Heaven has a nice golf course. Did I catch you at a bad time?"

"Nope, just cleaning up the mess." Molly patted the small stack of books. "Story of my life."

Molly's tone told me she wasn't *just* talking about the children of Matt Baker Elementary. Lucas was still fresh in her mind.

"I came here to apologize to you for what happened at dinner. I wanted to say something at the funeral, but it wasn't a good time."

"What do you have to apologize for?" Molly looked confused and even a little amused.

While she was dating Lucas, Molly was always at the house. I joked with her that she'd been adopted into the family and it was weird that she was fooling around with one of her siblings. She and I became friends, and I eventually saw her as something of a kid sister.

"Bringing Madison was a mistake." I leaned against the desk and crossed my arms. "She didn't know what she was talking about. She saw a moment to deliver a cutting blow to the opposition and took it."

"Opposition? Jesus… where did you find that woman?" Molly blew her air out and waited for a reply that I wasn't going to give. It didn't matter where I found her; all of that was over now. "What happened to Gloria? Everyone who saw you two together thought you were a perfect match."

"In true King fashion, I screwed that whole thing up." I shook my head slowly, focusing on the few trees visible through a nearby window. Why did thinking about that silly girl hurt so damn bad?

"Richard…." Molly studied the pain I tried unsuccessfully to hide from my face. "You're in love, aren't you?"

"I'm not sure I even know what that means." I still couldn't look at her. If I did, she'd see all my weakness laid bare, and much like my father, I hated when other people saw me like that. "Besides, it doesn't matter. I've been to enough contract negotiations to know when a deal is going south."

Molly chuckled. "You are the dumbest smart person I know, you know that?"

I blinked a few times to clear my mind and my heart; only then was I able to look at her directly. "How do you mean?"

"I know Gloria. We went to high school together. She's not a boardroom or a committee or—" Molly rolled her hand to help her find the words she was looking for. "—or rival corporation. Gloria is a living, breathing, *crazy* human being, like the rest of us."

"It's that obvious, huh?" I smiled weakly.

"Oh yeah." Molly laughed. "I know you've never fallen in love before, Richard, because you wear it on your face like a mask."

"I have to work on that."

"Love isn't a skill you can train. You can't go to seminars and get better at it." Molly was full-on in teacher mode.

"I'm going to have to. I screwed it up, Molly. Gloria never wants to ever see me again." I sat in a chair that was slightly too small for me. Now I fully felt like I was a little kid again.

"All right, answer me this," Molly said with a smirk. "Was she pissed at you last time she saw you?"

"*Very.*" I thought about the lucky, oblivious, college girl that now has a bottle of Glenlivet.

"Then she still cares about you." Molly picked up on my blatant look of confusion. "You were on her mind enough to be angry, dummy. If she didn't care about you, then seeing you again would've annoyed her, *maybe*. The fact that she was so angry at you means that there's still hope, if you want it."

I did. This kind of yearning was a foreign feeling for me. I wanted Gloria more than anything.

"Okay," I said, standing back up. "Be my consultant. I tried getting her a gift. Nothing as cliché as flowers, it was something I actually knew she'd like."

"It's not enough to truly *know* her anymore; now you need to show her that you deserve her."

"What do I do?" There was a subtlety to this, an art form I was extremely unfamiliar with. Getting women into bed with me was second nature. Pillow talk was a language I spoke fluently. This though, keeping a woman I couldn't live without was more difficult than anything I'd ever known.

"I don't know." Molly scrunched her mouth to the side of her face. She put a hand on my shoulder. "At this point, it might take a really big gesture. Whatever you do though, don't stop fighting for her."

How did this happen?

I came here to repair Molly's relationship with Lucas; it feels like it's the other way around. I pinched my cool metal cufflinks between my thumb and forefinger. A new resolve hardened within me. Molly was right; I cared too much for Gloria to let her go now.

"You give good advice for someone who doesn't take any of it." I was glad for all Molly's help, but that wasn't why I came. What happened at that dinner was my fault. I needed to be the one to make it right.

"Please don't." Sadness crept into Molly's face. I didn't want to hurt her, but there were things that had to be said.

"Dad's will, the competition, I know how bad all of it sounds." I snatched up a metal apple paperweight off the desk and passed it back and forth between my hands. "I've come to realize there's more to it than a dying man's fever dream. It's not about getting a woman pregnant. That is a big part of it, but that's not the spirit of what Dad was trying to do."

"Honestly?" Molly suddenly looked tired. "I don't care what the spirit of the agreement was. I just can't do it anymore. I've spent half my life waiting for Luke to do the right thing. I'm done waiting."

My teeth clenched and unclenched as I debated breaking an old promise. It was an important secret to keep at the time, but that time had passed. There was something Molly needed to know.

"No one knows this…." I put the apple down where I found it. This wasn't news you could deliver while idly holding something. "Lucas paid for all the school's renovations. I think it cost him everything he made off his albums. The only request he had was that they name the school after Matt."

Molly furrowed her eyes and walked to the window. She watched the last of the buses pull away to drop off their precious cargo. For a long time, she didn't say anything.

"Whenever I asked about the donor, I was told that it was 'a friend of the Bakers.' I wanted to thank them, but no one seemed to know any more."

"Lucas wanted it to be anonymous so it wouldn't take anything away from your brother. I'm only telling you because I think it's important you know how much he cares for you. Lucas loves you, Molly. He loves you more than I've ever seen one person love another."

The dull roar of a motorcycle pulled into the semicircle driveway the buses had left from. *Lucas,* I thought. *He'll never give that damn bike up. It's as much a part of him as his guitar.*

Then I heard several more bikes pull in.

"It's not about love," Molly said distantly.

I walked to the middle of the room and saw what she was looking at. Four men put their kickstands down in a no-parking area. They all wore black leather vests with patches on them. They were some kind of biker gang.

"What are they doing at an elementary school?"

"They're here for me," Molly said. There was something in her voice. It wasn't fear; it was *resignation.* It had an air of inevitability to it.

"Like hell they are." Molly was like the sister I never had. There was no way I was going to let anything bad happen to her while I was around.

"That right there." Molly flashed a small grin at my protectiveness. "Find a way to show that to Gloria, and she'll love you till the end of time."

"Molly—"

"It's okay." Her smile faded as she grabbed her purse. "The one in the middle with the beard is my husband. I called him."

"Husband?" My eyes opened wide enough to fall out of my head. I didn't know she was married. That didn't make any sense; Molly was never the cheating type. "Does Lucas know?"

"Yeah, they actually met briefly." There was a twinkle in her eyes when she said that. Something must have happened, and I was willing to bet it wasn't good. "Jason and I are separated. It's complicated."

"You weren't seeing him while you were with Lucas, were you?"

"No! Of course not. I'm not even seeing him now. We're just going to talk. Jason wants to make amends for… everything that happened."

I had such a bad feeling about all of this. Molly was going to ride off with a biker gang? It felt like I was trying to row up a waterfall. Everything was falling apart. I was hoping that if I could at least help Molly and Lucas get back together, maybe all of this hardship would be worth something.

"I don't know that guy, Molly." I stepped between her and the doors leading out of the library. "But I promise no one will ever love you like Lucas does."

"And I'll always love Luke more than anything." Molly smiled wistfully. "But I can't trust him to be there when I need him. I feel awful about saying all this, especially after everything with your dad."

Molly took a moment out of respect before continuing. "Jason made mistakes, some worse than others, but he was always there. I might not be in love, but at the end of the day, I know I won't wind up alone with a broken heart.

"Better the devil you know…."

"That is the stupidest damn thing I've ever heard." I couldn't hide my frustration. "Jason might be the devil you know, but that still makes him a *devil*."

Molly smiled at me, knowing I wouldn't understand, then crushed me in a great, big hug. "Goodbye, Richard."

CHAPTER 23

Lucas

Not him.

With white knuckles, I twisted the throttle on my bike and sped toward the fringe of town. I dangerously weaved in and out of traffic. On the best of days, the speed I was riding was borderline suicidal.

The sun had just dipped below the mountains, but most people didn't have their headlights on yet. There was enough light for me to ride, but not enough for me to be seen easily. It was the worst time for a biker to be on the road.

That's fine. One way or another, I wasn't planning to be on the road for long.

I had a woman to claim.

Not him.

It was a miracle no cops saw me. Even if they had, I doubted I'd have pulled over. I didn't give a shit about the speed limit. Not now, not when Molly was back at that MC clubhouse with *that* scumbag.

Richard had just arrived when I pulled into the clubhouse parking lot. He must have already been on the road when he called to let me know that his talk with Molly hadn't gone well.

He tried to talk me out of doing anything rash while on the phone, but the second he uttered Jason's name, I lost it. I hung up and raced over as fast as I could. There was only one thing on my mind.

Not him.

It was one thing for her to leave me. If she needed time and space to heal and get her life back together, I could respect that. I would wait for her as long as I had to, but I refused to let her go back to a piece of shit who *hit her.*

I parked my bike a ways down the sidewalk and hoofed it up to the front entrance, which was lined with nearly thirty bikes. *Full house tonight.*

Whatever. Bring them on.

I didn't care about anything else but finding Molly and kicking the shit out of Jason.

"Wait a damn minute!" Richard shouted from the other side of the road as he got out of his Aston Martin. He really hadn't had time to plan for this or else he'd have switched to a different car before coming over to this side of the tracks.

"I can't," I said, not slowing down. "I'm done waiting."

"Goddamn it, Lucas. Use your head!" Richard stood in front of me, trying to block my way. "If you walk in there and start a war, you're not coming back out in anything but a stretcher. Just wait until tomorrow and talk to her when she's not surrounded by angry bikers."

I stopped, but not because I had any intention of leaving.

Richard wore his dark three-piece suit and vest. He was clean shaven, his hair freshly cut and styled. He was a large guy, a little taller than me, and had a wall of gym-made muscles.

For as big as he was, it was obvious he didn't belong here.

This was a world of bar fights, knives, and gangs. It was rough, unforgiving, and occasionally life altering. This was a place for guys who looked like me—long hair, beards, jeans, T-shirts, and tattoos.

I might've been a rock star back in the day, but not anymore.

This was my world now.

"He *hit her*, Richard. Nothing's going to stop me from walking in there."

Richard pulled out his cell phone. "Let me at least call the police."

"For what?" I put a hand over it, blocking the call. Molly didn't report the assault when it happened. She didn't even have a bruise anymore. "They haven't broken the law yet, and you said she went of her own free will."

"Lucas...."

"I appreciate the concern, I do, but I have to do this." I clasped a hand on Richard's shoulder; then I stepped past him toward the door. "Go home, big brother. I don't want you getting hurt too."

I shoved the door open roughly, announcing to everyone inside I was here and I wasn't hiding. I didn't know what was going to happen next, but I did know she was about to see what kind of man Jason really was.

The bar looked no different than a hundred other dive bars I'd been to. There were tables and chairs strewn about, but most people hung out at the bar or played pool. The room was smoky with dark windows and had flags, posters, and other biker memorabilia all over the walls. It wasn't just filled with bikers either; there were hang arounds, ol' ladies, and friends of the club that didn't wear the uniformed black-patched vest.

I'd been in enough biker bars across the country to know this was on the tamer side. Granted, that was like saying it was a friendlier wolves' den. There might not have been one-percenter outlaws, but it was still a room full of large, angry men who I knew for a fact were armed.

And it was still very clear I wasn't welcome.

The classic rock music droned on, but the conversations in the room started dying out one by one as all eyes eventually turned to me.

I scanned the sea of leather and denim for Molly.

She sat in the back of the room drinking a beer; there was a look of disheartened resignation on her face. It told the world this was the best she was likely to do and that she had accepted her sad fate.

I could only imagine what he said to convince her that *this* was where she belonged—down in the mud with him.

It made me furious and sad.

"Listen, pal—" A younger member who hadn't got his full patch yet walked up to me and crossed his arms to look tough.

"Fuck off, prospect. I'm not here for you." I brushed past the kid and started walking toward Molly.

This is the time, I thought. *Molly needs me. It's time to fight for the woman I love, and God help whoever gets in my way.*

"Hey!" the prospect shouted after me, before his attention was pulled back to the opening door.

"I'm with him," my brother said, pushing his way past the leather-clad human speed bump.

Hearing Richard's voice made me smile and bolstered my resolve. Having him by my side definitely helped keep me focused when all the bikers in the room got off their stools or chairs and surrounded us.

"Who the fuck do you think you are walking in here like this?" Jason stood up from his shot at the pool table, but instead of putting the stick down, he gripped it tighter.

Jason was only a little older than me and already

had salt and pepper in his short-cropped hair and long beard. He was easily a little taller than Richard and about as wide as I was; the man was a freight train that decided to stand up one day.

"We met once in the parking lot." I flashed my teeth. It wasn't a smile, more like when a wolf peels back its lips before it attacks. "You might not remember me all that well on account of you being knocked the fuck out."

"You're that little bitch that sucker punched me!" Jason said, looking me over. He was sizing me up to see if he could take me in a fight. He had a few inches of height on me, but that was it. If this came to blows, it would get real messy and come down to who wanted the win more.

"And you're the weak prick that hits women," I countered. In a fair fight, I'd beat him, especially if I was fighting for Molly.

Thing was, there was no *fair* in a street fight.

There was a silence that fell onto the room. Most MC clubhouses I'd been to had strict bylaws against that kind of behavior. There was a muttering of disapproval or even disbelief that made its way through the crowd. It would take more than an outsider making accusations to sway a brotherhood.

"You stepping in here was the biggest fucking mistake of your life, asshole."

"No," I said, ignoring the man. I looked only at Molly. "The biggest mistake I ever made was not moving heaven and earth to get you back sooner, Molly."

Molly looked surprised and had lost some of that resignation that bogged her down.

Good. I never wanted to see that look on her face ever again.

"Hey!" Jason stepped up in my face. "I'm talking to you."

"Good for you." I stepped around him and walked to Molly's table. To my surprise, the bikers separated enough to let me pass. I guess more of them believed I was telling the truth than I thought.

I could feel Richard's tension growing as the bikers filled in behind us, blocking the exit. We weren't safe, not by a long shot. There was no backing out now. We were both in it until the end, however that may go....

"You shouldn't be here, Luke," Molly finally spoke up, adjusting her glasses.

"I shouldn't do a lot of things, Moll. But I can't just leave you again. I can't." I reached for her, but Jason grabbed my wrist.

"You should listen to *my wife.*" He wrenched me back to face him again. "Walk out of here right now. I don't want Molly seeing what I'm going to do to you."

"You can do so much better than this guy." I was in a locked stare with Jason but was still talking to Molly.

"And what, she deserves you? You're the piece of shit that abandoned her. I was there for her when her brother died." Jason shoved a finger into my chest.

"Where the fuck were you?"

I grabbed his finger and bent it back painfully, teaching him not to touch me. Each time he moved away, I'd twist against the joint, threatening to break the digit and stopping him in his tracks. After I made my point, I eventually let him go, then turned my attention back to Molly.

"Molly, I don't deserve you either. You are a beautiful, amazing person that deserves the perfect man, someone who will cherish you and never let you down.

"I've made mistakes, but I promise you I'm never going anywhere ever again. Even if it takes the rest of my life, I will learn to be that man."

"That's a nice vest you have there. American made?" Richard asked Jason, stepping between us to give me some room to talk to Molly.

"I'm so sorry for not telling you about the competition, but I will never keep anything from you again.

"Molly, I love you, now and forever. And if I have to fight a whole room full of bikers to prove it, I will." I reached out for her again, and this time Molly reached back.

Molly's eyes turned up and shined. She was starting to *really* see it. She was finally starting to understand that I meant every word, that I was willing to put my life on the line to declare my love for her.

And more importantly, she was starting to see that I

would never leave her again.

"Oh, Luke…." Molly smiled. "I—"

"Are you fucking kidding me?" Jason interrupted her and shoved the nearest biker in a rallying gesture. "This is my ol' lady, *my wife* he's talking to. I thought you guys were my brothers!" The grumbling in the room got louder. Technically, everything he said was true, but for all the wrong reasons. "Are you going to allow this *in our house?*"

"Jason!" Molly screamed to stop her ex-husband from attacking me while my back was turned.

I was too focused on Molly to see Jason slip past Richard. It wasn't my brother's fault; he was trying to keep an eye on dozens of people at the same time. Jason broke the pool stick across my back, which staggered me to one knee.

Molly called out again, but no one was listening to her or to anything anymore. The mob had been riled up. There were two men in their bar, who weren't in their club, causing trouble.

This place was about to erupt.

"Sorry about all this," I told Richard, standing back up. Back to back, we moved over into the middle of the room so that Molly wouldn't get hurt by accident. "I didn't mean to drag you into this."

"You did what you had to do. I can respect that." Richard turned his head to the side so I'd hear him over the room full of yelling. "But next time, try calling her first."

"I'll keep that in mind." I smiled, lining up my route that would bring me directly to Jason. "I'm going for Cannonball. You got my back?"

"Sure," he said hesitantly, raising his fists in a boxer's stance. "You take Jason. I'll take the other twenty...."

CHAPTER 24

A gnarly-looking older biker swung a bottle at my face. I dodged back and shoved him with so much force he left the ground and crashed against two of his friends.

I'll admit, when I agreed to help Lucas, I hadn't considered I'd be literally fighting his battles for him.

This was crazy.

We were outnumbered ten to one. Lucas and I were both big guys, but there was no way we were going to win this. Molly was yelling, trying to stop this madness, but her voice was lost in the drunk, adrenaline-fueled shouting.

Unfortunately for us, Jason sure knew how to get a crowd going.

Lucas and Jason were landing and blocking blow after heavy blow. I did what I could to keep people from blindsiding Lucas with a few kicks and punches, but I had my own small army to deal with.

I ducked a wooden chair as it broke apart against the wall behind me; the balding man who threw it looked familiar. Stepping back, I took a moment to survey the mob. I found that the balding man wasn't the only one that looked familiar.

Not everyone was lining up to fight us either. A few bikers near the bar were trying to ignore the whole thing. This group didn't strike me as having pacifists in their ranks, so why not jump in and overwhelm us?

Then I figured it out.

"Pete Tully, iron worker!" I shouted, pointing at one of the men at the bar. Then I pointed at another. "Joey Mills, dayshift manager at King Hotel."

I recognized some of these people from around town. They weren't fighting because they knew us, some even worked for my family's businesses. Joey had been the one to call and ask me to check on Lucas. *They knew my family.*

I stopped throwing punches, focusing instead on dodging and blocking. I called out the name and position of as many people I could recognize. Nothing slows a man down in a brawl faster than losing his anonymity.

For the people I couldn't remember the names to, or didn't know in the first place, I just called out the name of where they worked, and that seemed to be enough. Eventually the fighting died down.

"Jonathan Banks," I said finally, catching the fist that was meant for my face. The man looked shocked that I knew his name, caught his fist, and didn't immediately counter with a punch of my own. "How's your daughter doing in college—was it Jennifer? Jessica?"

I heard the girl's name only once in passing, while I was touring one of the King manufacturing plants with my father. My father made it a point to go to every place he owned and meet as many people as possible. The *People's King* they all called him.

When I asked him why bother? Why not just focus all your energy on expanding? He told me, *"The real secret to success is to take care of your employees. If you treat them fair and help them prosper, they'll work their asses off for you. A strong foundation in a skyscraper is far more important than the highest story."*

"Justine…." The buzzed man looked confused. I let his hand go, and he stumbled back a step. Once he got his bearings, he said, "Uh, good, she's doing good. Just started her sophomore year."

"I'm glad to hear that," I told Jonathan Banks, then turned to loudly address the rest room. "We're Richard and Lucas King. If you don't know us, then you know our father, William King. Some of you have met him; most of you have worked in one of his companies at some point."

"The fuck is all this?" Jason grumbled, getting back up from the floor. I didn't see what happened to him, but both he and my brother were bleeding from the fighting. Jason was holding a knife.

How long had he been using that?

Worried, I glanced at Lucas—who was still unarmed—to see if he was all right. Lucas had some cuts on his arms and a good slice running down his chest, but otherwise seemed okay.

One thing was for sure, this was getting too serious. I had to stop it before someone was killed.

"This whole thing is just a misunderstanding," I said, rubbing my battered cufflinks. "Caldwell Hope is our home *too*, our community as well! We're your neighbors. Our father helped *build* this town. Is this how you would repay him, by killing his sons? This is crazy. My brother and I came here to talk, not to start trouble."

"Bullshit!" a scarred, bearded man called out. "You fuck with one of us, you fuck with all of us."

"Damn right," Jason agreed. "You think you can come in here and steal my wife? Community?" Jason laughed spitefully. "You're not one of us. Go back to your glass mansions, rich boys."

"I'm *not* your wife," Molly said defiantly. Everyone quieted to let her talk. She walked up to her ex-husband and punched him square in the face. "You disgust me."

Jason growled and went to hit her back, not realizing the knife was still in his hand. My heart leapt into my throat as I watched Lucas step between them, shielding Molly. He was ready to take the full brunt of the stab.

Oh no.... I reached for Lucas but was too far away. I'd just lost my father; I couldn't lose my brother too.

At the last second, a beefy hand caught Jason's wrist, crushed it, and turned it out painfully enough that Jason dropped the knife. It clattered uselessly, then was kicked away.

"That's not how we do things here, Cannonball," said the gruff voice of a strong-fat man with long gray hair and a neatly kept mustache and goatee. The name patch on his vest read *"Hooksy. President."*

"I never worked for the man, but I *knew* Will King," the MC president began. When he spoke, everyone listened. "Caldwell Hope didn't want a chapter of the Black Chains to set up shop, even out here on the outskirts. They thought we'd be dangerous, bad for the community. Bring in drugs and all that.

"I fought for months to incorporate but got blackballed at every turn. That was until I got a call from some billionaire wanting a meeting." The president let Jason go, then shoved him away. "This ballsy motherfucker drove down to this very bar, back before we took it over, and talked with me for five hours. He wanted to get a sense of what we're all about.

"'The winds are changing in Caldwell Hope,' Will told me. 'With all the out-of-towners coming in, we're going to need some help keeping order until we get more cops.' In the end, we made a deal—he'd go to bat for us as long as we made this town a better, safer place.

"We both kept our end of the bargain. Without Will King, our chapter of the Black Chains wouldn't exist. As far as I'm concerned, the King family is as welcome here as our own."

"Pres, this piece of shit is trying to steal away my ol' lady." Jason thrust a finger at Lucas.

"I'm not your ol' lady, Jason. Not anymore. I came here to talk, but you were more interested in playing pool and starting a fucking riot than listening to anything I had to say." Molly turned to appeal to Hooksy. "I've served him with divorce papers, but he won't sign them."

"This true? You get served?" Hooksy glared at his Sergeant-at-arms, but Jason just looked away. The pres's hard features softened as he spoke to Molly. "Don't you worry about a thing; we'll get him to sign."

Hooksy turned to address the room one last time. "As for the rest of you! In honor of the passing of Black Chains honorary member, Will King, for the rest of the night all your cheap, shitty beers will be *free*."

The crowd roared in celebration, and the debris was mostly cleared. Jason brushed past a few of the drunker bikers, knocking one to the ground, then left muttering how he'd been betrayed by his own brothers.

The very same people who were just throwing fists and bottles at me came up to shake my hand and offer their condolences or wax nostalgic about their experiences with my father. Maybe it was because I wasn't all that familiar with the ins and outs of bar fights, but the whole thing was a surreal experience.

Lucas wasn't put off at all by any of it. He shook a few hands, but his determination was still clearly apparent. He was here for Molly and Molly only, through the bad times and the good.

He swept her up in a big hug and kissed her like it was his last day on earth.

It made me smile to see two people overcome all obstacles to be together. A stark, powerful melancholy washed over me as well as I thought about Gloria. Words couldn't describe how much I missed her at that moment. I wanted nothing more than to stare into those storm-cloud eyes and run my fingers through her fine black hair.

Watching Lucas swing Molly around as if they were the only two people in the room would've made it easy for me to be jealous of Lucas—after all, he got the girl and I didn't. I was beyond that petty emotion now though. I could honestly be happy for the two of them; they deserved both happiness and each other.

If anything, it doubled my resolve to make things right with Gloria. Love to me was a landmark picture on a postcard of a place I'd never been to. I knew it existed, but I had yet to experience it in person yet.

That was until Gloria.

Whatever she and I had together, it was too important to let it go without putting up a fight. I didn't know how I'd win her back yet, but I knew I would.

"Sorry to hear about the old man dying." Hooksy handed me a beer then extended a hand. "He was a bold, crafty sonofabitch. He will be missed."

"Thanks." I shook the man's rough, concrete slab for a hand.

It truly was amazing all the lives my father touched. It was funny, I felt more comfortable talking about my dad with this motorcycle club president than I did with some of my extended family. Hooksy had a genuine salt-of-the-earth quality about him that made me understand how these people could easily follow him as their leader.

I bet, despite their stations in life, he and my dad had a lot in common.

"I appreciate the save back there, Hooksy," Lucas said, with his arm around Molly. They were both all smiles and had a teenagers-in-love glow about them. "But if you were so buddy-buddy with our dad, then what the fuck took you so long, man? Your guys nearly took us apart back there."

There was a long, deliberate pause while Hooksy glared at my brother. For a moment, I thought the old biker was going to take Lucas's head off, until he snorted and chuckled.

"I was in the can," the president said, not losing any of his gruffness. "Next time call ahead first. Even your dad knew how to use a phone."

I gave Lucas a knowing look.

"Shut up, Richard." Lucas shook his head, smiling.

He gave Hooksy a lazy salute to show his respect and appreciation, then cocked his head toward the door. "Molly and I are heading out; we've got some catching up to do."

"Don't catch up too fast." The old biker smirked through his thick mustache, then shook Lucas's hand. Molly blushed several shades at the veiled innuendo and kissed Hooksy on the cheek.

"Did you know my father well?" I asked the old biker after the happy couple walked out the door.

"I did." He nodded thoughtfully, patting me on the shoulder. "He had the worst goddamn jokes I'd ever heard."

CHAPTER 25

Molly's apartment was a modest two-bedroom squashed between two other floors in her three-story building. It was a nice area and almost walking distance from the school she worked at.

"Well, being that you're too damn stubborn for a hospital, let me at least patch you up." Molly grabbed a first aid kit from her bathroom.

"How many bikers have you had to treat?" I marveled over the backpack-sized medical bag she had. "It's not that bad."

Each cut and bruise hurt like a bastard, but fortunately they were all pretty superficial, even the one down my chest. I was lucky that Cannonball was half in the bag when we got there, because if there's an unarmed person in a knife fight, it doesn't matter how good he is, that guy usually loses.

Molly laughed as she dropped the bag on the long, thin counter that separated the kitchen from her living room. "The fire department was updating the school medical supplies and had a few extra trauma kits, so they gave me one."

Molly clipped her hair back, washed her hands, then slid on a pair of disposable latex gloves. She let them slap against her wrists ominously.

"You're not going to ask me to bend over and cough, are you?" I teased, feigning fright.

"What kind of weird stuff did you get into while you were away?" Molly raised an eye, warily.

"Don't judge, it's been a long, lonely decade." I sat down at her small, expandable dining room.

"Whatever you say, Elmo." She smiled, then patted the air upwardly. "Strip."

"Yes, nurse." Instead of pulling the shirt over my head, it was easier to tear it the rest of the way and let it fall off my back. Bloody and naked to the waist, I waited for her soft, warm hands to take care of me.

Molly dragged over the only other wooden chair from her small dining room set and sat next to me. She carefully laid out everything she had, then got started cleaning me up with stinging antiseptic. Soon enough, everything was bandaged up. I only whined a little, not because the pain was overwhelming, but just to give her some playful grief. It was my way of showing her I was going to be all right. I didn't want her to worry about me too much.

"All set, you big baby." Molly peeled back her gloves and threw away the extra gauze and packaging. "I'll grab you some water."

"I don't need water." I grabbed her arm and pulled her onto my lap. "I need you."

"Luke…," she said, worrying about my wounds.

"I'm serious." There was no more silly playfulness in my voice, just awe and sincerity. "It's not every day you get a second chance at your one and only. You know I've always hated my stage name, but it's not until this very moment that I've ever felt so lucky."

Molly smiled deeply as her glasses slid down her button nose ever so slightly. I took them off and put them on the table. Her prescription wasn't too bad; she once described it as going from standard to high definition.

"I love you, Molly Baker." I kissed her. "I love you today." I kissed her again. "I love you tomorrow." And again. "I love you the day after that." And again. "I love you till the stars burn out and the sun falls from the sky. I love you to the end of our lives and to anything beyond that.

"I will never, *ever*, let you go again."

"Oh, Luke…." The worry fled from her tone, replaced by honey, nostalgia, and hope.

And love.

I kissed her again; this time it wasn't short nips. I drank in her lips like they were made of liquid heaven.

Heat climbed up my scalp as she ran her fingers through my hair.

There was nothing else to say after that.

I picked her up, carried her to her immaculately made bed, and gently laid her down. We tumbled into each other, careful around my bandages when we remembered. She rolled on top of me and tore off her layered, sleeveless blouse and cream-colored bra.

Her olive skin was flawless and perfect and just like how I'd remembered it. I grabbed her and pulled her close, needing to feel her skin on mine. I needed to breathe in her scent. It was all so important, so immediate.

I might have died somehow right then and there if I didn't get what I needed.

"I don't want to hurt you," Molly protested, but quickly gave in. Her eyes shared my same urgency.

"As long as I have you," I whispered into her ear, my lips playing gently against her lobes, "nothing can ever hurt me again."

Her body rippled against the vibrations of my words. I followed the shiver down her back with my fingernails. She turned her head to mine and bit then sucked on my bottom lip.

"Don't worry," she said between kisses down my chin and neck. "I'll protect you."

In a weird way, she already did. If she hadn't helped in the bar, who knows what would've happened?

Molly had risked everything and thrown away the

last ten years of her life. When it came down to the most important decision, she chose me.

In return, I showed her I was willing to die for her.

As she kissed down my neck, I got up to follow her, but she placed a hand on my shoulder and pushed me back down. "Uh-uh. You stay right there. Doctor's orders."

Her hard nipple grazed across one of my bandages, but I was able to suppress the sharp pain so she didn't notice. Fuck pain. The last thing I wanted was for her to stop. I could deal with pain. What I couldn't deal with was any part of her leaving my body.

When her tongue reached my collarbone, I became aware of how hard my cock was. She hadn't even got to my belt yet, and I was already making the leather strap groan at being stretched.

I let my head lull back and enjoyed the sensation of her licking over every one of my bulging muscles. When she hit my lower abs, I reached up and cupped her tits. I trapped her nipples between my fingers, rolling and squeezing them.

Her tits slid over the rough denim of my jeans, making my cock throb and yearn for her.

Molly roughly unfastened my belt and popped the buttons on my pants that took the place of a zipper. I sat up, straining against the pain from my wounds only to have her push me back to the bed.

"Down, stubborn boy."

I pulled my bottom lip out from my teeth and raised

my arms in submission. *You get to have your way for now, little girl.* "Go ahead, have your fun, but I'm coming to take what's mine soon."

Molly smiled, reaching into my pants and grabbing my thick cock. She squeezed, and a hot wave of pleasure tore up my core, making me moan. "Is that so?

Because from what I see—" She tore my cock out of my pants and breathed in sharply as if still shocked at how big I was. Her dark eyes narrowed seductively as she gripped tighter and began to work her hand up and down my shaft. The motion turned my moan into a grunt. "—I've got you by the balls, big man."

"Fucking hell…." I propped myself up on my elbows to get a better look at her. My cock was right next to her face, making it look so small in comparison. "I love you. You know that?"

"I think I can wrap my head around the notion." Molly winked, kissing the tip of my cockhead, before taking as much of me as she could into her mouth.

Her slick, pillowed lips and rough grip worked my rod over and over. She could only get about halfway down my shaft, but more than made up for it with the gymnastics her tongue was performing.

She was getting me close. I loved getting my dick sucked, but I didn't want to come like that with her. Not yet. I pulled my cock out and sat up.

"Hey," Molly protested, looking disappointed, then pouted. "I wasn't done."

"Too bad. Time's up. It's my turn." I was ravenous. I couldn't stand the fact that she still had clothes on, and in a painful whirlwind of motion, I had her dress pants and underwear thrown across the room.

"Luke, your arm."

A blossom of red darkened the bandage. I didn't care. It didn't look like it was going to bleed through, and there would always be time for more bandages later.

"I've got a spare just in case." With my good arm, I reached behind her and threw her down on the bed. Molly laughed at how easily my strong arms were able to move her.

I spread her legs and dragged the head of my cock over her glossy, hungry pussy.

Then, against every fiber in my body, I stopped.

"What is it? Are you all right?" Molly looked concerned.

"I'm not with you for any other reason than to be with you. I need you to know that. Fuck my inheritance. Fuck everything else."

"Luke...."

"Do you have any condoms?"

"No," Molly said with heaviness in her voice. When I started to pull away, she grabbed my cock, stopping me. "Let's do it."

"Are you sure?"

"We've lost so much time already. Let's start living, *really* living. I want all of it with you." Then she pulled me into her.

Her pussy scorched my cock and pulsed as I let myself be guided at first, then finished the thrust myself. The feeling was so different without the latex barrier, so much more intense.

It all felt so right, and for all the right reasons. We were really doing it.

"Oh God, that feels so good!" Molly moaned loudly.

I grabbed her thighs and roughly pulled them into me, throwing one of her legs over my shoulder. I was so much deeper inside her now.

Sweat rolled down between my pecs with the exertion. My body sharply reminded me of both Molly's pleasure and of the pain I'd endured. I pushed the latter out of my head and focused solely on her as I pumped forward and back.

Our bodies were different pieces to the same puzzle.

I lightly rubbed a thumb over her soaked clit, letting the waves of pleasure crash over her in time with my hips. Her pussy felt amazing. Being so close, so intimate, got me close to the edge.

I felt a tremor rip through her clit, and then her form went rigid. She bucked hard against me and screamed, *coming*.

"I love you too, Luke," she half breathed half screamed, and that was enough to make me explode. I emptied all of myself into her—all my love, all my hope, and maybe even our shared future.

I collapsed to the side of her, rolled onto my back,

and pulled her into a close snuggle. I never wanted her to be far from me again.

"Oh my God. That was…." Molly chuckled weakly, wiping the sweat from her hair-matted forehead. "That was something else."

"Yeah…," I said, basking in it all. Everything was so utterly perfect that it was hard to think of it as real. Then darkness crept into my mind; the one thing I hadn't told Molly began to eat away at me.

"What is it?" Molly asked, her head resting in the nook of my shoulder. She was very perceptive and must have picked up on my sudden distance.

No more secrets.

"I told you why I didn't come back, but not why I had to leave in the first place."

"Luke, that can wait. We don't have to talk about that right now." Her words reverberated through my chest.

"We do. I need this to be a clean slate between us. No lies, no omissions, and no half-truths." I craned my head over to kiss her on the forehead. "I want to spend the rest of my life with you, Molly. It's important that we do this right."

"I understand," she said softly.

"When my biological father, this guy named Nick, found out my mom was pregnant, he didn't want to give me up. Nick was a traveling musician who loved the idea of having a son of his own and was going to make a lot of trouble for Mom and Dad—custody battles, the media, the whole nine yards.

"Dad wanted to spare Mom the shame of a scandal hitting the news, so he paid Nick a bunch of hush money, but that wasn't enough. Nick wouldn't be happy unless he had some shared access to me. I don't know how, but Dad somehow convinced Nick to wait until I was seventeen and then I would go live with him for a year.

There was a discrete contract written up, and that was that."

"What was Nick like?" Molly asked hesitantly.

"I don't know. Apparently he died of a drug overdose when I was ten."

"Wait, so what happened? You didn't have to go?" Molly lifted her head to look at me, confusion in her eyes.

"That's what we all thought. Dad was so convinced that the problem went away that he never even told me I was adopted. Then my seventeenth birthday rolls around and Nick's *wife* shows up, contract in hand."

"What?" Molly's jaw dropped.

"Yeah. Dad tried to pay her off. He tried everything to get out of it. This lady wouldn't budge; she threatened to call the cops and the media. Mom had been gone for a year by then, so Dad ultimately left the choice up to me. Stay and Mom's reputation would be destroyed or go and the family avoids a massive scandal." My voice went quiet before I could bolster the strength to continue.

"But when you turned eighteen it was over. When you became an adult, you didn't need a legal guardian anymore. Why did you stay?" Molly asked.

"There was a loophole in the original confidentiality clause. It said that Nick couldn't tell the media; it didn't say anything about his spouse. When my original contract ended, I talked to my dad's lawyer and had a new one drawn up to extend that confidentiality to Nick's wife, but she wouldn't sign it without receiving something. I tried to pay her off but she wouldn't budge. She was a spiteful woman who just wanted to hurt the King family any way she could. She wanted time, not money. I negotiated her down to four more years and signed it as a legal consenting adult."

"Jesus...."

"I'm sorry, Molly. I didn't want to leave you, but I couldn't let this random person destroy what was left of my mother. Mom made one mistake in her life, and I couldn't let that overshadow every good thing she'd ever done."

Molly was silent for a painfully long amount of time. I felt nauseous. The thought of it all crumbling apart with Molly again was too much to bear.

"It's all right, Luke," Molly said, saving me from a fucking heart attack. "I forgave you today for everything that happened, *not just some of it*. What was this woman like?"

"Horrible. She somehow blamed my family for destroying her husband and wanted to take that anger out on someone. I was fed and clothed and treated well enough, but I was basically her slave for five years. When I got out, I heard you'd gotten married...."

"Why didn't you tell me earlier?"

"I couldn't. That was part of the contract; no one could talk about the deal."

"Jesus...." Molly hugged me as tightly as she could without mashing my bandages. "I'm sorry you went through that, and I'm glad you're back."

My heart soared. I couldn't love another person half as much as I loved Molly.

It had been one hell of a day. I went from the outrage of learning Molly was back with Jason, to fighting for my life, to winning her, to now.... My adrenaline was peaked, and my soul had never felt lighter.

We laid there for an hour, and all I could think of was "How long would things stay this good?"

Forever, I realized.

Our relationship would change and evolve over time. We'd grow old and experience the rest of our lives together. It would be this good in different ways *forever.*

Molly kissed me again, then rolled off the bed to start the shower. I turned on the TV for background noise and was about to join her when I heard the news.

"Several members of the band Deconstructed are in the hospital this evening after a serious car crash. Police say drugs may have been a factor...." The TV droned on.

Oh shit. The Deconstructed were supposed to play Gloria's store this Friday. There was no way that was going to happen now. Richard didn't tell me any numbers, but he did say that having them play there would make or break Black Rocket Records.

"You coming, Elmo?" Molly called playfully from the bathroom.

"Go on without me," I told Molly. I hated myself for turning her down, *especially when she was wet and naked*, but now my brother needed me. Considering how much he helped me make this happen, I at least had to try to return the favor. "I have to make a few calls."

CHAPTER 26

Richard

"So, like, is the show really canceled?" a passing teenager idly asked Gloria, who was standing on a stepladder, busily tapping liquidation sale signs to the exterior of Black Rocket Records.

Gloria exhaled with annoyed frustration, then resumed her work. "Yup."

"All merch, all records, F-ing everything is half off," read the signs she was hanging. Beneath that read, *"Tonight's show is canceled."*

"Oh…." The kid wandered off, not looking where he was going.

I grabbed the surprised boy by the shoulders to stop him from walking directly into me, then turned him and let him go. Without a word of protest, the hopelessly aloof teen ambled away.

I stood behind her for a moment, watching her. It was hotter than any late morning should be allowed to be. Gloria wore a gray tank top, a black baseball cap, sunglasses, and a skirt. Her shiny metal studs caught the light and accentuated her fair jawline and milky features.

I was instantly reminded how much I was attracted to her.

"Your signs have a typo," I said. "It says tonight's show *is* canceled."

"Oh for fuck's sake…," Gloria muttered, letting her forehead rest against the window. "You see the news, pal?" Finally, she turned to face the source of her newest pain in the ass. Seeing that it was me, her eyes flared excitedly for the briefest of moments, then immediately narrowed.

"What do you want, Richard?"

"I came to watch the show."

"The Deconstructed are in the hospital. How have you not heard the news?" Gloria turned out her palms dejectedly, then let her arms fall to her side.

It pained me to see the hurt in her face. Behind her tough girl act, I could tell that she was crushed. Her business meant the world to her, and now because some idiot musicians overdid it on drugs, she had to suffer for it.

"I didn't come for that show." I waved to the stretch limo parked across the street.

My brother exited the vehicle, followed by four

other men in dark shades who kept their heads down like those always on guard for paparazzi. I could only imagine the groveling, threats, and favors that were called in for Lucas to make this work, but somehow he did it.

Lucas did what every rock magazine in the country thought was impossible.

There was a stunned look on Gloria's face as each of the men said hi to her when they got close enough. Gloria took off her glasses as if the dark layer of plastic was lying to her.

"Hey, guys, this is Gloria Grant, owner of Black Rocket Records," Lucas said. He then turned to Gloria, a smirk splitting his face. "Gloria, this is John, Oscar, Isaac, and Robbie—"

"*Gunmetal Tears*…," Gloria blurted, then realized that was probably rude. She shook each band members hand in turn. "Shit. Hi. Sorry. It's nice to meet you! What are you doing here?"

"We're no *Deconstructed.*" Lucas shrugged, then winked. "But I'm pretty sure we can still draw a crowd. We'd like to play that empty stage tonight, if you don't mind."

"Are you fucking kidding me? Yeah, of course!" Gloria pointed inside with shaking hands. "Make yourselves at home. There's an office in the back you can hang out in if you want some privacy."

Lucas thanked her, then led his bandmates inside.

"How…?" Gloria looked at me, her rain-cloud

eyes sparkling. On the step ladder, she was nearly as tall as I was. She wasn't starstruck. It was what the band symbolized that made her hands shake. They were the last-minute, out-of-nowhere life saver that might keep her business afloat.

I smiled and said nothing. My words were stripped away by her beauty. If I could only see one thing for the rest of my life, I'd want it to be her face in this moment. I had never seen her so happy and relieved.

It made me want to devote myself to making her wear that look for the rest of her life.

"I thought they hated each other?" Gloria sniffed away her surging emotions. "After the thing in Berlin...."

"No, turns out they only hated Lucas. I don't think they're getting back together or anything, but they're at least taking a night off from being angry at my brother."

"Oh my God." Gloria carefully wiped the tears that threatened to ruin her black mascara. A renewed look of worry marred her perfect features. "The show... I canceled all the advertising. How the fuck are people going to know? Fuck!"

I placed a foot on her stepladder to keep her from toppling over as she suddenly jerked her phone from the waistband of her skirt. I quickly grabbed her hand, steadying it.

"Breathe," I said. "I've taken care of everything. You just say the word and every news outlet, blogger, and radio show in the area—*if not the country*—will hear about Gunmetal Tears one-night-only reunion show at Black Rocket Records."

"Why?" Gloria asked with hard, upturned eyes; this was all so tough for her to believe. I could see her difficult upbringing in those wounded eyes. It made my soul ache. "You don't even know me. Why do any of this?"

A million replies flooded into my head, but the only thing I could say was the most honest. "I don't know…. Because you're worth it. And because I was a fool to ever give you up in the first place."

Gloria crushed me in a hug I thought and hoped would last forever. She whispered, "Thank you," and began to cry.

"I'm sorry I'm not better at this. I've…." I hesitated. I felt stupid and vulnerable. I was always prepared. I mastered everything I set my mind to, but when it came to Gloria, I felt like a fumbling teenager, awkward and drunk off emotion. Then I forced myself to continue. I needed to say it as much for myself as for her. "I've never been in love before now."

"Stop making me cry, you jerk!" Gloria's chest heaved with laughter and sobs.

We stayed embraced like that until we became brave enough to finally look at each other. I'd never been so overwhelmed by emotion. I could feel that my eyes and nose were red. The remnants of smudged black rivers ran down her pearly cheeks. We were an utter mess, but at least it was honest.

On the sidewalk, late morning on a Friday, Gloria and I laid our souls bare to one another.

The band was inspecting the stage and fooling around when we came inside. A few customers hovered nearby, wondering if they were who they thought they were.

"Not bad, big brother." Lucas took one look at both of us and smiled from ear to ear. "Crazy, stupid love looks good on you." Then he turned to Gloria. "Once you pull the stick out of his ass, he's actually a pretty decent guy."

"Yeah, I'm beginning to see that." Gloria smiled at me in all her punk-rock glory. "Where's Molly? I feel like she had a hand in all this somehow."

"You're probably right. My girl is crafty like that." Lucas's eyes narrowed in feigned suspicion for a moment. "She'll be swinging by when school closes, so you'll get to ask her yourself later."

One of his bandmates called Lucas over to the stage. Before he left, Lucas shot me another look and a nod; the gesture said, *"Good job, man."*

"What happened to Ruthless Barbie?" Gloria asked when we were relatively alone.

"Who cares?" I said, frankly. It didn't matter what happened to her. I got the only girl I wanted. I then put my arm around Gloria, leading her to the office. "C'mon, we've got a concert to promote."

CHAPTER 27

Richard

The rest of the afternoon had gone seamlessly.

I had days to line everything up. My assistant and I went through all the preliminaries ahead of time. We'd prepaid for the ad spaces, had all the promotional copies written up, and had the band members record the various sound bites that radio shows would use.

I wanted everything to be as easy as possible if Gloria said yes.

Gloria didn't really have much to do aside from talking Judy down from a metaphoric ledge. Judy had learned the hard way that it was important to make informed decisions and not just jump into things half-cocked.

Gloria was right. Judy had a long way to go, but it seemed like she understood what was at stake now. Judy decided to take more of a back seat in Black

Rocket's decision-making process and even debated on enrolling in some small business management classes.

Then the fans came.

Word of mouth seemed to spread faster than the advertising, because people arrived in droves. It was a good thing that all the liquidation signs were taken down, because they weren't at all necessary. Inventory flew off the racks prior to the show starting. Gloria had to separate lines for cash and card.

Molly showed up just in time to be conscripted into helping ring people out. I wasn't spared either; I was given the cash-only line and a quick retail crash course. Even with the added cashiers, we still couldn't keep up with demand.

Well over half their total inventory sold out in hours; merchandise couldn't be brought out of storage fast enough.

An additional detail cop had to be hired last minute to deal with the massive amount of foot traffic and lines that stretched down the block. Everyone wanted to see this once-in-a-lifetime reunion show, and after a while, people were getting turned away due to reaching the building's capacity.

People lost their minds when Lucas took the stage to thank everyone for coming out. He was fully at home up there. His shirt off and his long hair unleashed, my brother was the quintessential rock star. With his bulging muscles and electric guitar, he looked more like a warrior than a musician. It was no wonder fans fell at his feet.

All things considered, it was amazing how well-adjusted he turned out where so many others had cracked under that kind of public scrutiny.

"Is this what you hoped for with the other band?" I asked Gloria loudly over the cheers of the rest of the band being brought out and introduced. The registers were all closed. The inventory was partitioned off and watched by private security. For all intents and purposes, Black Rocket Records became a nightclub.

"This is way better!" Gloria yelled excitedly, cheering along with the crowd. I loved seeing her this happy. She'd lost the cap and the shades hours ago, freeing her to jump around without dropping or losing anything.

Her shock of black hair whipped back and forth as Gunmetal Tears played their first song. I liked Lucas's band, but I was transfixed by Gloria. I couldn't take my eyes off her as she started dancing. Her arms pumped, her ass and tits bounced, and she sang along; Gloria exuded an aura of being absolutely carefree.

This was what was in store for me, I realized while watching her. It was all so strange and different. Her lifestyle lacked that safe sense of rigidity I'd grown accustomed to. For a moment, it was frightening, as most radically new experiences tended to be.

"Dance with me!" Gloria jumped into my arms and kissed away all my anxiety.

With her by my side, I felt indomitable, like I could

handle anything the world could throw at me. I'd always been confident and cocksure, but this was… something more.

I couldn't put my finger on it.

Gloria and I danced poorly and clumsily, and we didn't care; the whole point was just to move together. I couldn't remember the last time I'd had this much fun with a girl outside of the bedroom.

When was the last time I even danced?

The song ended, and I kissed her. I lost myself so fully in her pomegranate-flavored lips that I didn't hear Lucas calling for me. The spotlight had to fall on us for me to get yanked back down to the planet.

"Get up here, Richard," Lucas demanded.

I was hesitant, but only because I wanted to stay with Gloria. Gloria wasn't having it. She shoved me toward the stage to face whatever was coming my way. The crowd parted for me, and Lucas lent a hand for me to climb up on stage.

I thought I'd be giving some sort of speech, thanking everyone for coming out tonight and praising Gloria's store. Instead of all that, Robbie, the bassist, handed me his instrument. After Lucas introduced me, I protested that I didn't know any Gunmetal songs.

"But I know you know some Deconstructed songs. Looks like we finally made it to that talent show, huh?" Lucas smiled mischievously, slapped me on the back, then went right into the opening of one song I was pretty sure I remembered.

I was rusty as hell, but I got through it. I glanced up at Gloria whenever I could. She feigned swooning, and I instantly relaxed. I wasn't playing for the hundreds of people in and out front of the store; I was playing only for her.

Lucas played guitar and sang, even doing the back-to-back with me during one of the instrumental parts. The whole thing was an intoxicating experience, and before I knew it, I was strumming out the last few chords.

"Richard King, everyone!" Lucas called out, inciting the crowd to roar. I hopped off the stage and made my way back to Gloria; people patted me on the back and fist bumped me along the way.

Doing that made me understand my brother more. The screaming crowd, the noise, the lights, the satisfaction that came with doing everything right made me see why he'd chosen that path. I used to think it was frivolous, but experiencing it firsthand was thrilling. It wasn't something I'd ever pursue, but I loved watching Gloria's face light up during the performance.

"I do all right?" I asked Gloria after a big greeting kiss.

"You were great!" she yelled over the crowd as Oscar, the drummer, did a solo. "Let's go to the office."

I paused with Gloria at the door of her office when Lucas got back on the mic. It looked like he had something important to say.

"Before we get back to Gunmetal's greatest hits, I

want to do something special. I've been working on this one fucking song for months now, and I couldn't figure out the ending up until recently. You mind if I play it?" The crowd screamed excitedly, which was as close to a *"go ahead"* as he was going to get. "I'm still working on the title. So for now, we'll just call it… *Molly's Song."*

No shit…. Good for you, little brother.

Gloria pulled me into the office and closed and locked the door behind us. We were behind the speaker stacks, so the music wasn't as deafening. The office was big enough to house her and Judy's desks, a few extra chairs, and some overflow cases of inventory.

"You know my parents met in this very building. I guess it used to be a diner back in the day," I said, really liking the irony. It was hard not to imagine what life would be like with Gloria. There was a beautiful chaos that came with the thought of being with her.

"You're not going to ask to marry me, are you?" Gloria shot me a sly grin as she closed the blinds.

"That would be crazy." I carefully avoided the question.

"Good. Because I'm crazy enough to do something stupid." *Like say yes,* her eyes said. Gloria walked over, tearing off her tank top and bra.

"Is that so?" I pulled off my button-down and stepped into her embrace.

Our tongues searched the inside of each other's mouth as we passionately groped one another. I palmed, then grabbed her ass, squeezing tight enough for her to squeak. Gloria plunged a hand straight down the front of my slacks and grabbed my cock, and it fully harden in her hand.

"The cops can't protect you now." She smiled wickedly while stroking my massive length from inside my pants. She abruptly stole her face from mine and glared at me. Hand still on my cock, she squeezed threateningly. "I'd better not see another letter from you after this."

"I've made my decision," I said, liking the rough pressure she used on me. I clenched a fistful of her hair and pulled her head back so I could drag my tongue down her neck. "You won't be able to get rid of me that easily."

"Good," Gloria declared, releasing my belt and unclasping my pants with authority. It was easy to tell that she wanted this just as badly as I did. Was I on her mind as much as she perpetually invaded mine?

I moved her up against Judy's cluttered and overstuffed desk. I wanted to brush everything off it and pin her to it like I did with her counter out there but decided against it. Instead, I dropped into a crouch, grasped her inner thigh tightly, and wrenched down her soaked panties. They were hot to the touch.

Boy shorts, I knew it. I smiled knowingly.

"Hey!" Gloria feigned a little outrage to cover her mild embarrassment. "You were the last thing I was expecting today. Cut me some slack."

"I'll do more than that," I said, sliding my hand up under her skirt and cupping her smooth, wet pussy. The pressure of my hand lifted her up onto her toes and had her gasping in air.

My life for the longest time was control in all things, *even sex*. For the first time ever, I let passion take over. What was this woman doing to me?

Whatever it was, I liked it. No… *I craved it.*

With careful, deliberate ease, I split her lips and rubbed her swollen clit, before plunging two fingers into her and thrusting until her eyes rolled back in her head. She moaned my name. I had her in every way.

Gloria was wholly mine.

I stood back up, slipping my wet fingers into my mouth, and sucked them clean. "Mmm. Just like I remembered."

"Jesus…." Gloria slapped a hand on the desk because her knees were too weak to hold her.

I finished removing my slacks and boxers; my cock was rock-hard and eagerly glistening with precome. Being inside her and hearing my name lit my core on fire. I wanted every part of her; it was hard to even think straight.

"I'm still not ready. Y'know, for kids," Gloria said hesitantly. "Not just yet."

Was she afraid that I might leave her now?

Seeing how scared she was at the thought of losing me filled me with a warmth I'd never felt before. I'd been with so many women, but never anything like this. It was a strange feeling to know someone actually cared about me.

"I can't help you get your inheritance." The words tumbled heavily out of her mouth.

"It's just a number." I finally understood what my father was trying to say in his backyard when we had that first meeting. The realization boiled in my brain. The money didn't matter. It was who you spend it with that mattered.

"That's a pretty big fucking number. Really think this over. I don't want you to be disappointed that I'm not the girl you wanted me to be."

I took her face in my hand and gazed into those beautiful eyes of hers. "Gloria, you're still *all I see.*"

The wry expression on her face softened to a small accepting one. She nodded slowly, deciding to trust what I was saying. Then the corner of her mouth dragged up into a smirk and she walked over to the overflow inventory.

Gloria searched them and broke open one of the cardboard cases. Inside was a display set of the same plastic-wrapped condom boxes they sold in their novelties section. She ripped and shredded until she was finally only holding one sealed condom.

"Please don't tell me that glows in the dark." I groaned at the thought.

"No, that's dumb." Gloria whirled around with a growing smirk and then pressed something, and the condom began to buzz. "These vibrate. Feeling adventurous?"

My eyes opened wide as she sauntered over to me.

"Usually I don't pull out the sex toys until the fifth date," I said, knowing full well I've never been on any *fifth dates.*

"Spoilsport." Gloria kissed me, then clicked off the buzzing. She wiggled her fingers playfully, which was when I noticed the plastic ring. The condom didn't vibrate at all; it was the ring. Gloria was a bit of a joker; I'd have to remember that.

She rolled the thin latex down my cock. When it was snug and secure, she zapped the tip with her ring.

"You're asking for it now," I said, sweeping her up in a bear hug. She screamed and laughed as I laid her on the throw carpet in the center of the room.

Her ring was still vibrating, so I grabbed her fingers and grazed her clit with them.

"Oh fuck!" For several seconds, she writhed underneath me, her pussy bucking against the sensation. Gloria went from biting her bottom lip to her mouth opening into an O wide enough to fit my cock. Mercifully, I eventually pinned her offending hand to the carpet.

I teased the head of my cock against her slick petals. Each time I threatened to dip into her, she raised her hips toward me. She screamed in frustration, "Oh my God, you're the worst! Fuck me already!"

My cock throbbed as the waves of heat rolled off her wet, ready pussy. Finally, I couldn't stand it any longer and pushed in. Even through the condom,

Gloria felt unbelievable.

After everything we'd been through, it was hard to imagine actually having sex with this woman. It was like when your whole dream was spent building up to a moment, but you always knew you'd wake before you got to the payoff. I expected to just wake up at any second, sweating in my bed with a massive hard-on.

That wasn't the case as I buried every thick inch of my shaft inside her. I slowly pumped, pinning both her arms to the carpet. God, I loved the way she twisted and twerked beneath me. Her thighs and legs gripped me tight, threatening to never let go.

That was fine by me.

"Oh fuck…." Her pale form panted and crunched forward as little earthquakes rocked her. Gloria's moan turned into a series of joyous screams that would've been heard throughout the entire store if a rock band hadn't been playing just outside.

My head swam as she climaxed. She became a full-body vice around my cock and ripped the orgasm out of me that had been building since before I'd been arrested. I mashed my hips into her, sliding her up the carpet a few inches, and filled the condom with my thick, milky seed.

Every second of being inside her was incredible. Even after coming, when my cock was rapidly growing sensitive, I still didn't want to pull out. I hovered over her, kissing her. It was the eager, sloppy kisses of two teenagers making out desperately.

"Tell me something," I said. Sweaty and exhausted, I touched my forehead to hers. "Your eyes, are they really that storming shade of gray?"

"Yes." I could feel Gloria getting self-conscious. "I used to wear brown contacts to keep kids in my high school from making fun of me."

I looked at her, but she'd already glanced away. Gently, I raised her chin so I could see into her furtive eyes. Gloria was so strong and confident in so many ways that it was easy to overlook her vulnerability.

"Children can be such fools," I said. "I have never seen eyes more beautiful than yours. You're perfect in every way, Gloria, and I want to spend the rest of my life telling you that."

Gloria reached up and dragged me down beside her before starting to cry.

"I think I've waited my whole life for you," she said. "How's that even possible?

"I don't know, but we have all the time in the world to figure that out."

The music had finally died down. Lucas's muffled but still audible voice took the mic once more.

"I'd like to give a special thank-you shout-out to my brother, Richard and his beautiful girlfriend—the creative force behind Black Rocket Records—Gloria," Lucas howled. He then smugly added, "You may have heard them through the wall earlier."

I laughed. Gloria covered her face in embarrassment as the crowd cheered. *Jesus…. How loud were we?*

"Thank you all for coming," Lucas continued. "We love each and every one of you. If you had fun, tell your friends! That's our show, good night!"

EPILOGUE

My parents' house was way too big for us.

It'd been a little over a month since we moved the rest of Molly's stuff in, and we still had no idea what we were going to do with all the extra rooms. This place was a palace. For as frivolous as I always thought it was, this house was the one I grew up in. I had so many good memories here.

The best memories were of my time spent with Molly.

One night after we'd moved in, we snuck up to my old bedroom and fooled around like when we were kids. We both loved the idea of keeping the house in the family, especially with Molly pregnant. The thought of raising our own children where we'd grown up was a really nice feeling.

"Have I ever told you that I love you?" I slipped

behind her as she was chopping vegetables and kissed the side of her neck.

Molly was my rock. I had spent so much of my life being carried by the wind that it was so nice to finally belong to something. She was my tether to the world. I'd never been more creative than I had these past few months, and it was all because of her.

Gunmetal Tears never got back together, but that didn't stop me from writing new music. Knowing I had Molly by my side made the words and notes gush out of me. I'd have a full studio album recorded and mixed by the time little Reese was born.

After the world heard Molly's song on YouTube, record executives were banging down my door to get me to sign with their label. Richard toyed with the concept of starting up our own label—King Records.

I think he enjoyed being on stage at Gloria's store more than he'd let on.

"Maybe?" She smiled, pondering thoughtfully. It had almost been twelve hours since I last said it to her. "Although… I think I'm due to hear it again."

"I love you."

"How much?" she demanded, sliding off the chopped carrots and grabbing a crown of washed broccoli. Dinner was done save for a few appetizers that were just finishing up.

"I love you more than there are germs on a ten-year-old's hands."

"Wow." She turned and kissed me. "You love me an

awful lot."

There was rapping on the door, followed by a loud greeting.

"We're in the kitchen!" Molly yelled, much too close to my ear. She laughed apologetically when I recoiled; then she kissed my ear. The popping sound at the end of the kiss only made it worse. "Sorry, Elmo."

"Your love hurts." I smiled indignantly, then turned to greet Gloria and my brother. They brought a bottle of sparkling apple juice for us all to share.

"Holy shit, look at his cute little nose!" Gloria rushed over to the fridge where the ultrasound pic was posted. She clammed up suddenly, then ducked down and rubbed Molly's stomach. "Sorry, little guy, Auntie Gloria was a sailor in a past life."

"That's all right." Molly laughed, and they hugged. "It'll break up all the classical music we subject him to."

"Hey!" I said, jokingly defensive, shaking Richard's hand. "I read that was important for a kid. It helps them grow up smarter."

"If that's the case, Molly," Richard added with a grin, then clasped a hand on my shoulder, "considering who the father is, your son will need all the help he can get."

"Funny." I shoved him. It really was incredible how close he and I had become these last few months. It was hard to recall why we hated each other so much in the first place.

"After months of back and forth about the inheritance, I received this letter from Dad's attorney this morning." Richard pulled out the sealed envelope from his breast pocket. He hadn't opened it yet, probably wanting to wait until we were all together. "There was a note with it, explaining that there was an intentional delay set into the reading of the will as per Dad's instructions… for some reason."

"Dad should've gone into acting." I snatched the letter from my brother and tore it open. "He was the most theatrical person I've ever met."

Molly dried her hands and joined me at the breakfast nook table. We all sat down, ready to hear whatever words of wisdom Dad wanted to impart.

"My boys," I started reading Dad's letter out loud.

"First of all, I want to apologize for all the subterfuge. Despite what you may think, it was never my intention to cause either of you any anguish. I love you both more than life itself.

As a parent, I wanted nothing more than for you both to thrive and find your own happiness.

As your *parent, I knew the only way that was going to happen was if I pit you two against one another. That fierce competitive spirit has brought you both so much success. It's also what tore you both so far apart. Competition is a good thing, but it's only half of the coin; the other side is cooperation and coming together.*

The challenge was issued because you both were so damn stubborn—a family trait, I'm afraid—I couldn't simply tell you all that. In order for you to truly understand, I had to show you.

I had to let you figure it out on your own.

This competition, the heartache, the trials, the reward of inheritance... none of this was for me. Unfortunately, I knew I would never survive long enough to see my beautiful grandchildren, but that didn't stop me from wanting you to experience that joy.

My biggest regret in life was not spending the time I had left with the people I cared most for and not valuing those people enough while they were still alive. That was a mistake I never wanted to pass down to either of you.

However, at the time of my writing this, I can see that you're both going down a dark, lonely path. That frightens me more than you know. I've seen the hollowness that waits at the end. My only hope now is that neither of you have followed too far in my footsteps.

That was my final lesson to you.

You are too old for my fatherly wisdom. In truth, you've both far surpassed me in your own ways.

Richard, you are a far better CEO than I was at your age. You have the uncanny ability to break problems down and knock them over like dominoes. You will do great things for the King legacy. Our corporation could not have a better leader. Please understand that you are more than your net worth. Find yourself outside of the company as well. You are a man first, a King second, and everything else afterward.

My nurse tells me you've been seen with a plucky, young entrepreneur and that you look happy. You keep your emotions locked away too deeply; you need someone to bring that out of you. I hope this woman is the key to unlock that vault.

Lucas, I can never repay you for the debt you willingly paid on behalf of your flawed parents. Fulfilling that insane contract and living with that other family for the sake of your mother's honor was the noblest act I have ever seen. You weren't of my blood, and by not managing the family business, you broke a King tradition hundreds of years old. Your boundless empathy showed me that blood and tradition were nothing before family and love. Pursue whatever makes you happy, my boy.

I'm saddened that I never had the chance to get to know Molly like my wife did. However, seeing you together recently made me understand why your mother always turned a blind eye to you sneaking *her over when you were children. She would say to me, 'You wouldn't deprive an arm of its hand? Lucas and Molly completed one another. They belong together.' And she was right.*

Please don't be sad for me. I'm with your mother now and all the pain is gone. I couldn't fathom a better place to be.

Lastly, this competition will stay in place until the terms are met. Fall in love, have children, find happiness.

I'm incredibly proud to have called you my children. I love you both.

Signed, William, an old fool, who learned far too late that being a father was what truly made him a rich man."

The heavy silence in the room that followed was broken only by soft sobbing.

"Looks like you won, little brother." Richard hugged me. "Congratulations. The inheritance is yours."

The victory sank in my stomach like a hot rock.

Richard and Gloria were planning on having kids eventually, just not right now. They wanted to explore the world together and nourish their passions for entrepreneurship. They shouldn't be punished for not falling in love faster. If I took all the money for myself, I'd truly have learned nothing.

No, it couldn't end this way.

"I'm not a very good millionaire, let alone billionaire," I said, wiping my eyes and addressing the group. "With the way Richard and I have treated each other over the years, neither of us deserve this money."

"What are you saying?" Richard asked.

"Let's step out of the long King shadow for a while. We're all doing fine with our own ventures; we don't *need* the fortune. I'm saying we give it all to our kids when they're old enough."

"It'll be a present from their grandparents," Molly said, her beautiful red-rimmed eyes glistening with hope.

"I like the idea of that, little brother." Richard put an arm around my shoulder. "Let's let the burden of tradition skip a generation."

"You do realize that means we're all going to have to put up with each other for the next few decades, at least." Gloria smirked, clearly enjoying the idea.

"I'm instituting a King dinner night! We're going to practice being a family." Molly beamed with ideas of future events. I loved her so damn much. "Tonight can be our trial run, what do you think?"

"I'm down. And as Dad would say, 'If it's worth doing once....'" I looked at Richard expectantly with my own smirk.

"Really?" Richard sighed, placing his hands on his hips. I nodded. "Fine. *It's worth doing a thousand times.*"

EPILOGUE 2

Richard

HALLOWEEN MASQUERADE PARTY

"Fuck." Gloria's storm-gray eyes nearly rolled out of her head at the sight of the ring. She almost dropped her glass and silver mask. I had them commissioned at the same time; our masks were really one full face mask that was split in half.

Two halves of the same soul.

"That wasn't really the effect I was going for." I raised an eyebrow, looking up at her from my bent-knee proposal. My own mask was placed on the carpeted floor next to me. I wanted to do this later on in the evening, but odds were that we wouldn't be alone like this again.

The Halloween masquerade was on full tilt in the

ballroom next door. Gloria and I were in an adjacent room that was almost as big. Muffled music, dancing, and laughing could be heard through the wall. Candelabras and flowers filled the room with exotic scents and mysterious, uneven lighting.

A few guests that cut through this room hushed their conversations when they saw me on one knee. There was a sensation of awe and wonder everywhere, except the only place that mattered, directly in front of me. Could I have misread our relationship? Was I moving too fast for Gloria?

Maybe this was a mistake. I began to stand up.

"Wait!" She pulled her mask off and reached a hand out toward me. "Shit, I'm sorry. You caught me off guard. Can we start over?"

I smirked, settling back down on my knee. I was again reminded why I loved this woman so much. Gloria was so unapologetically genuine. She always kept me on my toes, or in this case, off them.

"Gloria Grant," I started again. I raised the box containing the engagement ring I bought. The ring—like her—was very special and extremely hard to find. I finally opened the box and let her see the modest yet rare artifact. "Will you marry me?"

"Yes!" Gloria choked out the word, trying not to cry and failing. She tightly wrapped her arms around me like she had fallen off a boat and I was the life preserver thrown in to save her. There was a quiver in her voice that warmed my bones. "Oh my God, yes!"

After a dozen tear-stained kisses, she let me go long enough to actually *look* at the ring. I couldn't hide the pride I felt in getting her one I knew she'd like.

"Holy shit. Is that…." Her bottom lip quivered. "Missy Gladstone's ring!"

I nodded, smiling.

Gloria had turned me onto her favorite band Twilight Son. They were a three-piece ensemble from the seventies. The bassist married the drummer early in their career, and they both died in a plane crash ten years ago. It took a lot of money and time, but I was able to track down the original engagement ring.

"You are amazing!" Gloria wasn't the type of girl to squeal, but she came awfully close as she held it up to get a better look at it. "How?"

"That doesn't matter." I picked her up easily. I might tell her about the whole arduous process someday, but not now. I wanted her to remember today as the day she became engaged, nothing else.

"Y'know, you don't have to do this," she said, blotting at her cheeks to not spread her mascara further. "You already lost the bet."

"I won something far better than an inheritance," I said, ignoring my vibrating phone. No one was going to take me away from this moment.

"You are so goddamn cheesy." She smiled broader than I'd ever seen before. "I love you so damn much."

"I—" My phone hadn't stopped vibrating. I took it out of my pocket, intent on throwing it across the room when Gloria stopped me. She looked up at me and told me to answer it. "It's my assistant."

"Go." Gloria rubbed the deep maroon of her lipstick off my lips and cheeks. "I need to put my face back on and gloat to Molly anyway. You'd better come find me when you're done."

"Nothing could keep me away." I kissed her long and passionately, ruining what was left of her lipstick. "Remember to wear your mask. This is a masquerade after all."

Gloria sighed, frowning. She did her best to tolerate the party's theme. She loved the mask but didn't love actually wearing it.

I slipped on my masquerade mask, straightened my tux, and went to the kitchen.

There was an argument with one of the chefs and some administration noise for me to clear up, but soon enough everything was running smoothly again. I made my way through the dance hall to find Gloria.

"Hell of a ride, huh?" Lucas had stepped off stage and grabbed my shoulder. He'd been chatting with the band while they set up for their next song. His long hair fell all around the black skull mask he wore. He nodded toward the table where Gloria, Molly, and Judy sat. Gloria was showing them the ring. I couldn't suppress the happiness I felt at seeing the excited smile sweep across her face as she talked about it.

Every time I looked at her, I felt warm all over.

"I used to think we were cursed to always come out

on top but never win," Lucas said, slowly shaking his head at his pregnant wife and burgeoning new family. He still had trouble accepting that this wasn't just a really good dream he'd wake up from. This was his life now.

"Yeah." I threw an arm around my younger brother and jerked him to the side roughly. Because of our competitive natures, our brotherly love was always rough like how dogs played. "Dad would've finally been proud." I shook him. "Don't screw it up."

"Speak for yourself, old man." He flashed me a grin, nodded, then broke away as the band started to play the song he wrote for Molly. In true Lucas-style, he parted the crowd and slid on his knees to the table our women were sitting at.

I walked over like a normal person, when an argument across the hall caught my attention. Judging from the size and shape of the man getting yelled at, I knew right away that it was NFL MVP Garrett Walker. I hadn't met him, but I remembered seeing his name on the guest list my assistant forwarded me.

I didn't envy that poor bastard right now; his wife was really laying into him about something. It wasn't any of my business, I decided. I had more important matters before me, like a fiancée to dance with.

"The trick to a masquerade party is to keep the mask *on*," I said to Gloria with a smirk. She only humored me with this party. She never liked a lot of pomp and ceremony.

"Oh my fucking God!" Gloria roared, tearing the mask off and slapping it on the table. "There. Now it's *on* the table."

Judy and I laughed. Judy must've been giving Gloria grief about not wearing the mask either.

"Hi, Judy." I smiled warmly to her. "Do you mind if I steal my future wife for a dance?"

Judy looked great. She wore a light blue dress with a beautifully homemade mask. This sort of event definitely appealed to her; it was a shame she couldn't share this with her boyfriend. From everything Gloria told me about Doug, Judy was too good for that complete waste of space.

"Actually," Gloria started. There was a look of concern on her face that bothered me. It made me wonder what Judy's boyfriend fucked up *this time*. "Judy and I were in the middle—"

"I don't mind at all," Judy said in her customary, chipper, upbeat voice. She stood up and offered a little smile before walking toward the dance floor. "I need to go find Doug and harass him into at least one dance before he gets too drunk and makes another scene."

"Everything all right?" I asked, watching Judy leave.

"I don't know." Gloria's lips pulled to one side of her face in a confused frown. "I'll talk to her tomorrow.

How about you? You put out all the fires?"

"We're all right." I looked down at Gloria's hand. It looked so fucking good with that ring on it. "What'd they say?"

"They didn't even know who Twilight Son is! Can you believe that? I have the worst friends." She smiled despite herself. She was still excited to be wearing it.

When the song ended, my assistant took the stage and called out for me to come take the microphone.

"Please tell me you didn't set up some grand gesture that would put me in the spotlight in a room full of strangers," Gloria groaned.

"No, of course not," I said, texting my assistant to cancel the announcement. Gloria saw through my lie and smiled. I stood up and grabbed Gloria's hand. "Okay. You caught me. Let's get out of here before they find us."

Gloria laughed, no doubt reminded of the last time we were at this golf course for a party. I guess we'd never get through a whole night at one of these events, and honestly, that was fine by me. As long as she was by my side, I couldn't care less about these parties.

I led her out of the main hall, down a few large hallways, and into an audio visual supply closet. Not the most romantic of locations, but at least no one would find us here. Eventually they gave up on the announcements and the band resumed. Even at this distance, I could still feel them playing through the walls and floor.

"I think we've lost them." She laughed, panting from our quick exit and light jog.

The room was small, cramped, and stuffed with electronics. The terrible, cold, overhead fluorescent lighting made Gloria look even paler than she usually did, but it still couldn't rob her of her natural beauty. The flickering light also deepened her thunderstorm eyes, making her seem even more mysterious.

I would have the rest of my life to explore everything about Gloria, I realized.

"What is it?" she asked, noting my broad smile.

None of the answers that swam to the forefront of my mind could convey how blessed I felt at that moment. Nothing I could say would capture the way I saw her and how much I loved her.

So I kissed her instead.

My lips went on a tour of her neck and ears. I dragged my teeth down her soft, pale skin. With one hand on the middle of her back and one cradling the back of her head, I pushed her against the wall hard enough to make electronic equipment on the nearby shelves rattle.

We fell into each other.

Gloria let out a heavy erotic sigh and began wrenching at the lapels of my suit. She liked the edge of roughness. I liked giving her what she wanted… after a bit of teasing.

"You know," Gloria said between smiling and spikes of breath as I worked my mouth down her collarbone, "people are going to wonder where you are."

"Let them." I tugged the zipper down the back of her black dress and worked my other hand behind the loosening fabric. With a quick snap of her bra clasp and a shrug of her shoulders, all the fabric fell to the floor.

Gloria was naked save her panties, low heels, and a devilish smile.

I gasped in air at the sight of perky tits and hardening nipples. She was so damn perfect. A wave of near-incontrollable lust boiled inside of me, making my cock ache from the sudden blood rush. A moan escaped me as I licked my lips and scoured every inch of her soft, glowing skin.

Gloria's dark eyes deepened when she saw the hold she had on me. I couldn't imagine ever wanting anyone else than her, and she knew it.

I loosened my bow tie as she slid my jacket off and unbuttoned my shirt.

I pulled off my sleeveless fitted undershirt and watched her eyes light up at the hard rows of my abs and chest muscles. Like a moth drawn to my fire, her hands were on me, sliding over my every carved valley and solid ridge.

"I've always wanted to fuck in an AV closet." Gloria smiled as she pulled my belt free with a sudden jerk and smoothed my pants off my hips, letting them fall to the ground. The thick, rigid outline of my hard cock strained against my tight black briefs. Gloria bit the corner of her lip when she caught sight of it. "High school me would be so impressed right now."

"High school you couldn't imagine how hard you're about to come. Not in her wildest dreams." I swept everything off a nearby cabinet and sat Gloria down on top.

Flat-screen monitors crashed around me and fizzled against the concrete floor. A few shards of glass and plastic sprayed over my pants, ripping small holes in the fabric. That didn't matter. Seeing her like that made it impossible to think straight. All I cared about was peeling her panties back and diving into her pussy.

"Oh yeah? You'd be surprised at—oh!" Gloria laughed and quivered as I jerked the thin cotton fabric aside.

As horny as I was, she was lucky I didn't tear her underwear in half. I pulled her thigh up to open her slit even more. Gloria's pussy eagerly glistened. Her whole body wanted me. I couldn't contain myself anymore. I ravaged her clit and lips with a savage hunger.

"Holy shit!" Gloria arched her back and pushed her hips into me harder. She loved the pressure of my tongue and teeth against her tender petals. I licked and sucked and teased and flicked until her thighs began to tremble.

I slipped my free hand into my briefs, squeezed my rock-solid cock, and began to stroke myself as I ate her out. She quivered, like champagne bubbles rising to the top of a toasting drink.

"Fuck, fuck, fuck, fuck." Gloria twisted to the side as her first orgasm rippled through her. "Don't… don't stop."

I slowed my tongue but didn't stop. I dropped my briefs and let my cock bounce in the open air. I loved knowing that she was watching me. Hearing her moan made me jerk off faster, which in turn caused her to moan even louder.

"You've ruined it for me now." The vibrations of my deep voice sent shivers through her pussy. "I'm never going to be able to stroke my cock without the taste of your sweet pussy on my lips."

Gloria nearly bent in half as another orgasm made her gasp in air.

When all the aftershocks subsided, I leaned away from her, wiped my chin, and stood up. Gloria pressed a hand into her chest, trying to slow her heart rate. She was nearly out of breath. She grabbed the back of my neck and pulled me in for a kiss. She licked my chin and, smiling, said, "Good."

Gloria hopped off the cabinet. The broken monitors crunched beneath her heels. I wheeled a cart of projection equipment out of the way and laid my jacket over the concrete. Then I brought her down on top of me. I could feel broken bits of plastic and glass poking me beneath my jacket, but I couldn't care less.

Gloria straddled my legs just above my knees, bent down, and licked the length of my cock, then kissed the tip sweetly. "I don't think I'll ever get tired of this."

"I sure as hell hope not." I shot her a concerned sidelong glance.

"Not this." Gloria smiled and squeezed my cock in both hands like a joystick. The pressure felt amazing. I was so big that she needed to use two hands to get fully around it. She started to stroke me as she continued. "Of us. Of being with you. Every day, I wake up and have to remind myself that it wasn't all a dream. We're actually together, and now we're even getting married! I thought it would be too much. I… I was worried I might run away from it all. But now I couldn't imagine being anywhere else in the world."

I sat up as best I could and pulled her face close to mine. "You are my world."

"I even love how cheesy you can be sometimes," she said through a wide smile.

I laughed, knowing I could never allow myself to be vulnerable enough to be corny around anyone else than her. *My fiancée.*

She pushed me back down and began sucking me off. Her mouth and tongue worked their magic along my cock. I thought about sliding into her tight, hot pussy, but I didn't bring any condoms. We might have children eventually, but we weren't ready for it yet.

That was fine. I loved the way she sucked my cock.

She moved her hands up and down my shaft in time with her mouth. Occasionally her lips would pop off my hat head with a loud smack, so she could draw in air. She felt incredible. I couldn't touch myself half as good as she could.

It wasn't just her skill that made my heart beat ring out like rain on a tin roof, it was *who* she was. She was going to be my wife.

She rolled her tongue around the tip of my cock and massaged my balls. That was it. I grunted and propped myself up on my elbows as my whole body contracted. Hot cum shot down her throat.

Gloria struggled to swallow all of me, but she got through it. She even licked me clean afterward. I loved seeing her tongue drag long, slow lines up my thick cock, even if the light pressure after such a big release was almost too much to bear.

I grabbed her and pulled her down on top of me. "I love you. Did you know that?"

"Somewhere between my first and second orgasm, I figured that out," Gloria said, with her head pressed to my chest. She smiled after a moment then added, "The engagement ring also helped."

I stayed quiet, hugging her tightly and basking in the weird, beautiful moment.

"Do we have to go back out there, Richard?" Gloria asked, a slight whine creeping into her voice.

"Fuck it, let's just stay here."

"All night?" She lifted her head and gave me a skeptical but amused glance.

I brushed the matted, sweaty, black lock of hair from her brow and looked into her incredible, stormy-gray eyes for what felt like a lifetime. "As long as I'm with you, Gloria, I don't care where I am."

End

ABOUT THE AUTHOR

Jackson Kane is a professional stuntman, athlete, romance author, and above all else, a hopeless romantic. From American Ninja Warrior to some of your favorite films, Jackson brings a unique writing style forged from countless harrowing adventures.

He's a lover of travel, his fans, his romance author peers, dulce de leche, and all things beautifully weird and interesting. He invites you to relax, have a pisco sour, and let him thrill and excite you in a way no other author can. Jackson will show you what the world looks like through the eyes of a genuine Bad Boy.

Come with him, and…

DARE TO READ DANGEROUSLY

ABOUT THE PUBLISHER

Hot Tree Publishing opened its doors in 2015 with an aspiration to bring quality fiction to the world of readers. With the initial focus on romance and a wide spread of romance subgenres, Hot Tree Publishing has since opened their first imprint, Tangled Tree Publishing, specializing in crime, mystery, suspense, and thriller.

Firmly seated in the industry as a leading editing provider to independent authors and small publishing houses, Hot Tree Publishing is the sister company to Hot Tree Editing, founded in 2012. Having established in-house editing and promotions, plus having a well-respected market presence, Hot Tree Publishing endeavors to be a leader in bringing quality stories to the world of readers.

Interested in discovering more amazing reads brought to you by Hot Tree Publishing? Head over to the website for information:

WWW.HOTTREEPUBLISHING.COM